Title: Matthew Unstrung
Author: Seago, Kate
Book Level: 5.4
AR Points: 7.0
Quiz #: 20121 EN FIC

D1539573

MATTHEW UNSTRUNG

MATTHEW UNSTRUNG

⁂ *by Kate Seago* ⁂

Dial Books / New York

Published by Dial Books
A member of Penguin Putnam Inc.
375 Hudson Street
New York, New York 10014

Designed by Nancy R. Leo
Printed in the U.S.A. on acid-free paper
First Edition
1 3 5 7 9 10 8 6 4 2

Library of Congress Cataloging in Publication Data
Seago, Kate.
Matthew unstrung/by Kate Seago.
p.   cm.
Summary: A 17-year-old boy who has suffered
a mental breakdown in the early 1900s is able to regain his
sanity with the help of his brother.
ISBN 0-8037-2230-3
[1. Mental illness—Fiction. 2. Clergy—Fiction.
3. Fathers and sons—Fiction. 4. Brothers—Fiction.] I. Title.
PZ7.S43773Fi 1998
[Fic]—DC21   96-50159   CIP   AC

For Karl and Lynnette

Acknowledgments

To Terry, who cooked—and who believed.

To my family, who told my grandfather's story.

And to Clifford Whittingham Beers (1876–1943),
whose courageous 1908 autobiography,
A Mind That Found Itself, taught America
about mental illness.

CHAPTER

The boom of the pipe organ enfolded the students in the chapel like a warm quilt. Morning sunlight, diffused through the stained-glass windows, colored the dusty air with pastels.

"Onward, Christian soldiers,"

(The hypotenuse of a triangle is equal to . . .)

"marching as to war,"

(. . . the sum of its legs no that isn't it I'll . . .)

"With the cross of Jesus"

(. . . never figure this out my father will . . .)

"going on before. . . ."

Eight hundred well-scrubbed Anglo-Saxon faces turned toward the choir loft for the closing hymn; eight hundred teenage voices joined as one.

In the second row seventeen-year-old Matthew Hobson shook off the geometry problem and held his hymnal lower. He watched the valves on the huge organ pipes, arrayed along the wall above the altar, open and close in time with the music.

This was the part of the service Matthew liked best: the music filling the chapel, the organ bass more a physical sensation than sound, the voices of his classmates surrounding him.

The chapel itself reflected the sturdy traditions of the midwestern Protestant churches that had paid for its construction. The pews were built of dark hardwoods, but they had no ornamentation or carving. Simple velvet drapes hung on either side of the organ, hiding the tiled baptismal font on one side of the dais and the choir robing room on the other. Mounted on the wall above the choir loft was the hymn board, showing in changeable panels the hymn numbers for the morning's service and, at the top, the date: September 23, 1910.

As the song ended, Matthew slipped his hymnal into the book rack on the back of the pew in front of him. The rack also held a Bible for each student—not that any of them would have dared to forget his own. The hardwood rails along the front of each rack had been drilled with a row of holes that now held each student's emptied Communion glass.

"Come with us for cherry phosphates after chapel?"

whispered Matthew's best friend, Cappy, nudging Matthew in the ribs.

Matthew shushed Cappy, hoping the chapel proctor hadn't noticed. Matthew didn't need any more trouble with the administration right now.

"How about it?" Cappy persisted.

"Have a class," Matthew whispered.

"Suit yourself, Preacher," Cappy whispered back, nudging Matthew's ribs again.

Matthew glanced up at the choir loft to see the proctor scowling at him.

Matthew Hobson was the sort of young fellow grandmothers pointed to with pride. After years of parental prodding, he stood very straight, which made him seem much taller than he was. His eyes were alert to everything around him.

Women saw those eyes and wanted to mother him. Men met his gaze and shared confidences; Matthew was the trusted repository of most of the school's whispered adolescent secrets. But Matthew had few close friends, and now that he was the one who needed advice, he was pretty much on his own.

He worried as he walked back to his dorm. His grades were falling again despite days spent in the library and nights hunched over his study desk.

Matthew had been at Priory Bible College in

Nebraska for two years. He studied harder than anyone else he knew, but still barely made grades high enough to keep him in school. The problem, his father wrote, was lack of application to the task.

Maybe so, Matthew conceded, although he thought he was applying himself too thin as it was.

It wasn't the long hours he spent studying; actually he enjoyed the pure academic challenge, the give-and-take of information. His studies, especially art and music, intrigued him. He loved school, and until he had come to Priory, he'd always done well.

But as he'd explained to his father when he was home last summer, now that he was at college, he found that he couldn't concentrate, couldn't internalize the ideas his professors were trying to teach him. He could parrot back the information, but he couldn't do anything with it.

And there was something more, a problem that he could never broach with his father. He had barely begun to admit it to himself: His schoolwork was taking him ever closer to graduation—and ever closer to a ministry of his own. And even though Matthew and his father had planned for it all his life, even though he had thought he wanted it with all his heart, he found himself paralyzed to make it happen.

Matthew spent more hours sitting in front of his

textbooks, but he found that the longer he sat there, the less sense the words on the page made.

The only time he left his studies was for work. Although his father could well afford to pay for his education, the Reverend Mr. Andrew Hobson felt that Matthew's earning his own tuition would build character. So each day Matthew spent the three hours between his last class and evening chapel selling Canterbury illustrated Bibles and *The People's Home Library* door to door.

Matthew was shy, and it was uncomfortable to have to introduce himself to somebody new at every door. But it was wonderful being out in the fresh air, walking around the trim little college town with his leather satchel full of books. Most people were nice to him, and he was enjoying the first flush of independence from earning his own money.

The sales had been going well, and Matthew, strolling toward the lecture hall, decided he could relax a bit for the next few weeks.

With nearly every moment taken up by either work or studies, walking had become his only time for reflection. Matthew was annoyed when his reverie was interrupted by a raucous car horn.

A sunflower-yellow farm truck was parked next to the curb. Against it leaned Matthew's older brother.

"Hello, boy!" Zack called out.

Matthew ran over to the truck. He and Zack roughly shoved each other back and forth, yelling, and ended up in a bear hug.

Zack had always been Matthew's hero. Zack was five years older than Matthew, and stronger and taller. He was good at sports, popular at school, and handsome in his own lanky way. The main resemblance between the brothers was in their straight noses and large hazel eyes. But although Zack's eyes were as big as his kid brother's, they were touched with worldliness.

"This yours?" Matthew asked, pointing at the shiny new truck.

Zack nodded. "Yeah. I'm going to drive it back out to Colorado."

Matthew walked around the new truck, running his hand along the bright fender.

"Let's go get something to eat. I want to talk to you," Zack said.

"Can't. I have a class," Matthew said.

"Ditch it. We need to talk."

Matthew laughed. "You'll get me expelled!"

"Could be the best thing that ever happened to you," Zack said softly as he pulled an envelope from his pocket and handed it to Matthew. "I did it."

Matthew held the envelope carefully.

"Open it."

This was the other dream, one Zack and Matthew had shared ever since Matthew was small. Late at night Matthew had crawled under the covers of Zack's tall bed, and Zack had read to him by candlelight from dime novels he had secreted between his mattresses about bank robbers and cowboys and Indians. Zack's whispered tales fueled Matthew's fertile imagination, and soon the boys were planning a ranch of their own "out West."

Zack had really done it.

Matthew put his Bible on the truck seat and gingerly opened the envelope. Inside was a property deed and a photograph. His eyes moved to the names on the deed. Zach had added Matthew's name.

"It's half yours," Zack said. He tapped his finger on the photo. "Him too."

Matthew turned the photo over and saw a massive bull standing in a corral. The bull's head was lowered aggressively, his eyes staring out of the photo at Matthew.

"That's Adonis," Zack said. "Not much personality, but the cows think he's beautiful."

Matthew grinned, then was suddenly serious. "But Father expects me to . . ."

Zack slammed his fist against the truck. "Don't! I don't want to hear it again."

Matthew looked crushed. Zack's expression softened.

"Look, Matthew, we've talked about this since we were kids. Now, are you coming with me?"

Matthew stared at the deed. He felt trapped. He handed Zack the paper and stammered quietly, "I'm going home at Thanksgiving. Maybe I'll talk to him then."

Matthew averted his eyes.

"Sure, boy," Zack said.

They stood together for a moment, trying to get past the awkwardness.

"Are you doing any better here?" Zack asked.

"I'm trying my best," Matthew replied.

"Which means no," Zack said, ruffling Matthew's hair. "If you need me . . ."

"I'll be all right," Matthew said unconvincingly, holding out the photo of Adonis.

"No, you keep it," Zack said. He hugged Matthew good-bye. "If you change your mind, Colorado is due west. I'll send a ticket anytime you say."

Matthew just shrugged.

Zack reached inside the truck, fiddling with some knobs on the dashboard and flipping switches and levers. He tinkered inside the engine compartment under the seat for a few moments, then pulled a crank from behind the seat. As he inserted the crank in a slot in the truck's side, Zack looked up to see Matthew watching intently.

"You want to try starting it?" Zack asked.

"Really?" Matthew asked.

"I told you—it's half yours." Zack climbed into the driver's seat as Matthew took his place at the crank.

"Before you crank it, you have to set the spark, open the choke, and advance the ignition. You saw?"

Matthew nodded.

"All right," Zack said. "Now you crank it with one smooth motion. Got that?"

Matthew nodded, concentrating.

"Watch yourself. It can kick back. Once saw a man get his arm broke doing this."

Matthew nodded.

Zack smiled and stepped back. "Go to it then."

Matthew set his feet, grabbed the crank, and turned it clockwise with both hands. But when the crank caught at the top of the arc, Matthew hesitated. The crank reversed, throwing Matthew backward. He landed on his butt, feet flailing.

Zack laughed as he helped Matthew up. "I told you to be careful, boy. One smooth stroke. Don't let it hesitate."

Zack leaned against the steering wheel to watch as Matthew squared himself at the crank.

"Don't hesitate," Matthew repeated under his breath.

Matthew gave the crank a powerful turn, but the crank went full circle without catching the engine. Matthew, off balance, fell forward this time.

"I give up," Matthew said as he got up and dusted himself off.

Zack climbed down and walked over to help him. "No. You don't."

He stood Matthew at the crank again. He made a little twirling motion with his finger and grinned as he readied himself behind the wheel again.

Matthew looked down at the crank in his hand, and his grip tightened. He closed his eyes and gave a mighty shove.

The engine sputtered to life.

Matthew, startled, opened his eyes. Zack tweaked the dials and levers, coaxing the engine to purr.

Zack put his arm around his brother's shoulders. "Sure you don't have time to go for a ride?"

"I have a class . . ."

Zack's eyes twinkled. "You can drive it."

"Yeah?" Matthew said in astonishment.

Zack motioned for him to get in on the driver's side. Matthew scrambled into the right-hand seat behind the wheel as Zack got in on the left.

"Let's go," Zack said as he engaged the gears.

Matthew gave it some gas. The truck jerked once, then lurched away from the curb and down the tree-lined street toward the ice cream parlor.

It was well past three when Zack dropped him off and Matthew walked, preoccupied, through the opulent dormitory lobby. His dorm room was messy with books, tennis rackets, clothing, and the general clutter that indicated teenagers lived there. School pennants decorated the wide-striped wallpaper.

Cappy reclined on one of the two beds, reading.

"I thought you were playing tennis," Matthew said in surprise.

Cappy jumped to his feet. "Let's go. Connie is waiting for us, and she's bringing a friend for you."

"Can't. I have to study," Matthew said. "I've lost practically the whole afternoon as it is." He took the photo of Zack's bull from between the pages of his Bible and handed it to Cappy.

"Boy, you've been holding out on me," Cappy teased. "Who's this delightful new creature in your life?"

Matthew snatched the photo back.

"You just missed Zack. He's in town, buying cattle for his ranch."

"He finally did it? That's great! When are you going out to Colorado?"

Matthew shrugged. "I want to finish school first."

Cappy threw his hands up in disgust. "Who are you kidding, kiddo? You'll go back east, just like your father wants. You'll be ordained, just like your father wants. And you'll wind up associate pastor of his church, just like your father wants."

Cappy took the photo. "The closest you'll ever get to this is when you order a steak dinner." He tossed it on the desk.

Matthew opened a book. "I have to study. There's a theology test tomorrow."

Cappy shook his head. "Your loss, old man. The ladies await!" He picked up his tennis racket, slung it against his shoulder with a flourish, and left.

Matthew grabbed a decorated "Atlantic City" pillow from the chair and threw it at the closing door. Then he carefully put the photo of Adonis back in his Bible and turned to his lessons.

For the next two weeks it became Matthew's habit to awaken in the hours before dawn to read one more chapter, to review a passage one more time.

Matthew and Cappy settled into a pattern: Matthew, in his nightshirt, would shuffle to the desk and pick up the last book he had been studying before

Cappy had forced him to go to bed. The scraping of the desk chair on the hardwood floor would rouse Cappy from under his mountain of blankets, mumbling, "Oh, come on, Matthew. Give it a rest."

Matthew never looked up once he had settled in at the desk. "Go back to sleep, Cappy," he would reply as he absently turned pages. As Matthew focused the lamp on his work, Cappy would put pillows over his head and tent the blankets still higher to block out the lamp for the few remaining hours before dawn.

Matthew didn't dare let his eyes close. Once asleep, without his endless studies to distract him, his mind would take him back to a day in his childhood—but not to a gentle afternoon in his mother's parlor or a morning visiting parishioners in his father's big black carriage.

At age six Matthew had swiped the keys to the church office from his father's big desk and carried them around all day, enjoying the heavy, important clink in his pocket. That afternoon, he had sneaked back into the study to return the keys just before his father was due home. He had reached into his pocket, but the keys weren't there.

As he stood at the desk, horror washing over him, he had heard his father come into the study behind him.

In his waking hours Matthew couldn't remember

what had happened next. But when he dreamed it, he always woke up screaming.

Then the headaches began. Matthew's vision would tunnel down until it felt as if he was wearing blinders. The dull, thudding ache would begin at the base of his neck and come crashing around to his eyes. He could only lie writhing in agony on his bed.

Cappy consulted *The People's Home Library*, the thick volume that Matthew sold along with the Bibles. The book, published by the R. C. Barnum Co. of Cleveland and featuring Barnum's own likeness on the frontispiece, combined a library of practical books: *The People's Home Medical Book* by T. J. Ritter, M.D.; *The People's Home Recipe Book* by Mrs. Alice G. Kirk; and *The People's Home Stock Book*, a compendium of veterinary medicine by W. C. Fair, V.S. It weighed twelve pounds.

Cappy found Nervous Headache listed under "Diseases of the Nervous System" in the medical section. " 'Nervous headache is a very common trouble and may be caused by over-doing or excitement,' " he read. " 'It is common among school children. . . . Poor health, worry, trouble and want of sleep are some of the many causes.'

"This sounds like you, Preacher," he told Matthew.

Matthew flinched at the nickname. "So what's the remedy?" he asked from the bed, his eyes rimmed red.

"I've been telling you to get some rest—and to let me get some," Cappy said.

"I mean medicine," Matthew said, getting up and taking the book from Cappy.

"Belladona, it says," Cappy replied. "That's strong stuff."

"Too strong," Matthew said.

"It says Coffea too. That's just coffee."

"My father would have a fit if he caught me drinking coffee. To him it's just like hard spirits."

Cappy took the book from Matthew and put it back on the shelf. "Then what are you going to do?" he asked.

"Pray that it goes away."

His schoolbooks, askew where he had left them on the bedside table, were the first thing Matthew saw when he opened his eyes on the morning of his midterm examinations.

It was daylight. It shouldn't be daylight yet.

Matthew grabbed the alarm clock. The winding key for the alarm was slack; Matthew had slept through the clatter until the alarm ran down.

Panic flooded through him as he realized that his

theology exam started in fifteen minutes—on the other side of the campus.

He leaped out of bed. Five minutes later he was fully dressed and racing down the dormitory staircase, books under his arm.

The campus was crowded, and Matthew had to dodge students and faculty as he dashed across the broad lawn to the theology building. He slid into his seat in the lecture amphitheater just before the proctor closed the big wooden double doors.

The professor glared up at Matthew.

"Just under the wire again, Mr. Hobson," the professor said coldly. "Very well. Let's begin."

Matthew opened his notebook, avoiding the instructor's eyes.

"This will be one half of your final grade for the term," the professor said to the class.

The student next to Matthew handed him a stack of test booklets. Matthew put one on the desk before him, then passed the stack down. He took a fountain pen from his pocket and folded his hands over the booklet. He could feel the headache taking hold again.

"Begin," the professor intoned.

Matthew's focus on the test page blurred. He sensed kaleidoscopic movement just beyond his peripheral vision. A thousand unfamiliar voices murmured softly, wordlessly above a background of weird music.

He shook his head to clear the distressing sensations from his mind and bent to the test.

Matthew was buffeted by his growing troubles, much as the campus was now raked by autumn winds. But he persisted through sheer willpower, even against all the distractions Cappy could think up.

"Hey," Cappy said one sunny afternoon, "my cousin Alberta came out from New York. Connie and I need you for mixed doubles."

Matthew made a face. "It's too cold for tennis. . . . Alberta? Is that the one with the warts?"

Cappy grinned. "Only little ones. But they don't affect her backhand."

"I think I'll just . . ."

"Yeah, I know. You'll just study," Cappy said. He swung wildly with an invisible racket and danced jauntily out the door.

Near the window stood two square oak tables. Cappy's was piled high with half-finished themes and a jumble of textbooks; most of the books still looked new, although the term was more than half over. Mixed in were concert programs, a glove, candy wrappers, scraps of sheet music, and a lady's hair comb.

Beside it Matthew's desk was clean, his inkstand at the top left corner and a lone geometry book squared with the top edge. A few magazines were neatly stacked on the shelf below.

Best to get it over with, Matthew thought with a sigh. Okay, start from the beginning. What *is* a hypotenuse anyway?

He flipped through the pages. Okay, there it is: the side of a right triangle opposite the right angle.

He pulled out a notepad and sketched a triangle. He circled the angle at the base, then drew an arrow to the long line connecting the horizontal and vertical legs. Okay, that made sense. Now, what was he supposed to do with it? This had something to do with the Pythagorean theorem, whatever that was. Okay, here it is. The square of the hypotenuse of a right-angled triangle is equal to the sum of the squares of the other two sides.

Why can't I remember that? he wondered.

Because I don't understand it, he answered himself. The words were meaningless.

How had this happened? He'd been in class every day, taken good notes. Matthew needed this class to graduate. The future he and his father had so carefully planned for him depended on his deciphering the mysteries of geometry and trigonometry and, after that, advanced algebra and calculus.

If only geometry were easy, like music or art. There seemed to be no rhyme or rhythm to this, only rules to follow. And apparently if you missed one, you missed it all. Matthew felt as if part of his mind was actually resisting the information all the while he was willing his brain to retain it. The mud was getting deeper and deeper.

He turned in the book to a sine table. And suddenly he had no idea what to do with it; he didn't even understand what question he was supposed to be answering about the triangle he'd just drawn.

Worst of all, the realization was beginning to sneak up on him that he no longer cared. The idea both liberated and terrified him.

For the first time in months Matthew took time to gaze out the window. Below him he could see the tennis courts where Cappy was defending his side of the net alone. On the other side were two girls in tennis whites.

Matthew recognized Connie Reever, a pretty red-haired girl with whom Cappy had fallen instantly in love. Or more like lust, Matthew thought smugly.

The other girl had the heavier build of a future farm wife, her hair in thick rope braids. That was Alberta, Cappy's New York cousin. No, thank you, Matthew decided.

As he watched, Connie hit a strong serve right past

Cappy's head. Cappy ducked, and the game collapsed as the three players dissolved in giggles.

Matthew went back to his books, but through the window he could still hear the laughter from the tennis court.

Finally he pushed his chair back, picked up the geometry book, and went for a walk. As often happened these days, he found himself strolling along the river.

The river path was bordered by pastures on one side, by the water on the other. Matthew stopped to skip a rock across the flowing surface, disturbing the water bugs and sending shimmering circlets back to the bank.

A bit farther on he found a cow straining her neck to reach through the fence to get at a last clump of grass, greener by the water's edge than in her pasture. Matthew pulled the clump for the cow and watched her chew it placidly, her eyes closing with pleasure.

He sat down under a nearby tree and opened his book. Within minutes he was asleep, lulled by the wind and birds and the soft rhythmic river.

The housemother for Matthew's dorm was Mary McWorthy, a solid Irish grandmother who had taken over the dorm five years before—just a year after her husband, a brakeman for the Union Pacific, had been killed in a train accident.

Mrs. McWorthy mothered the college boys as she had mothered her own children, who were now long grown and gone. She fussed after the boys to do their homework, to eat regular meals, and to get to bed by the decent hour of ten.

Matthew was a particular favorite of Mrs. McWorthy's: so polite, so quiet, such nice manners. But she worried about him. He was always so serious, and he never seemed to get enough sleep.

She was alarmed when the note came from the office of the Dean of Men. The letter was sealed; of course, Mrs. McWorthy would never have dreamed of opening it. She put it on the sideboard beside the door and glanced at it constantly during the morning, her other eye on the door.

Matthew finally came in, steadying a tall stack of library books under his chin. Mrs. McWorthy heard the door open and came out from the kitchen to meet him.

"A note came for you this morning, Mr. Hobson," she said in a worried tone.

Matthew carefully gave a slight nod. The stack of books swayed crazily.

"Please slide it on top, ma'am," he said, trying hard to hold the books in place.

Mrs. McWorthy wedged the note under Matthew's chin, and he tottered up the stairs.

"I hope it's not bad news," Mrs. McWorthy called after him.

But Matthew knew it was.

He put the books on his desk and sorted them, laying the note aside. He busied himself for the next half hour: He changed his clothes and washed his face, then carefully arranged his study materials. But when he ran out of things to do, the note still lay on the desk, and with a sigh, he tore it open.

Please call upon me at your earliest convenience.
George Anders, Dean of Men

Matthew picked up his jacket resignedly and headed across campus, his dread mixed with relief that his struggle was finally, terribly about to be over.

Matthew knocked and entered the impressive book-lined office. Dean Anders was a small man, nearly hidden behind the massive desk.

"Mr. Hobson?" the dean asked as Matthew entered.

"Yes, sir," Matthew acknowledged.

"Sit."

Dean Anders waved Matthew to a wing chair facing his desk, then picked up a sheaf of papers from the desk and gave them a cursory look.

He fixed Matthew in a sterile gaze.

"Your examination papers, Mr. Hobson. Do you know what they show?"

"No, sir," Matthew said miserably, although he knew full well the contents of the folder.

"Three *D*'s and two *F*'s, Mr. Hobson," the dean intoned.

Matthew sat very still.

"No response, Mr. Hobson?" the dean asked. He rose from his chair and came around the desk to stand directly in front of Matthew.

"My father wants . . ." Matthew began.

The dean cut him off.

"Mr. Hobson, your father and I were good friends when we both were undergraduates at this institution. You come from good stock. I therefore can conclude only that you are either willful or lazy, because I know you are not stupid."

He moved close to Matthew's face to continue. "Neither trait will be tolerated. Is that understood?"

Matthew nodded automatically.

"You will be expected to raise these marks to acceptable levels by the end of the term. Is that understood?"

Matthew again nodded, his body taut with anxiety. His hands clenched and unclenched against the arms of the chair.

"Yes, sir," Matthew mumbled.

"Good," the dean declared. "You may go, and I hope this is the last such interview we shall have."

Matthew went to the door. "Sir, will you be writing to my father about my marks?" he asked, exhaling the words quickly.

"At this point that is your responsibility, Mr. Hobson," Dean Anders said sternly. "We shall hope that events will improve, so that it does not become mine."

"Yes, sir. Thank you, sir," Matthew gasped as he escaped the office.

CHAPTER

Shrouded in early winter mists, a passenger train chugged through the grubby company towns, headed east.

Matthew stared out the window, textbook abandoned in his lap, watching the factories belching smoke into the leaden sky. The trees were bare of leaves; a recent snow had nearly melted, leaving gray slush at the roadsides.

The train car was shabby and crowded. Matthew tried once more to concentrate on his book, but the boys behind him were shoving each other, jostling Matthew's seat. Matthew turned again to the window.

The train was passing over a river. Through the struts of the iron bridge, Matthew could see the dirty water below. Everything was monochrome, dead. He turned back to his book.

The sun was nearly down when, three hours later, the train pulled into the small brick station at the edge of Brookbend, Wisconsin.

Brookbend was nestled into a shallow valley in the northern forest, at the edge of the great prairie. The town had been established in the late 1600s as a stop on the French fur routes into Canada and had enjoyed a reputation for pleasure, drink, and wild doings.

This past had, by 1910, been conveniently forgotten; the town fathers now marked the start of Brookbend from the arrival of a wagon train of two hundred good, sober Ohio farmers in early 1836.

The farmers who now controlled Brookbend's commerce and the town council were mostly descendants of those first stalwart folk who took over the original outpost from the soldiers and fur traders and created a town around their new farms on the upper slopes of the valley. In the first decade of the new century, they had already brought in electricity, telephones, and plumbing for their homes, street lamps and trolley cars, and a shiny new courthouse where they voted Republican at every election. The citizens of Brookbend were early risers who took their churching seriously every Sunday and put money in the bank every Friday.

As the train pulled in, Matthew scanned the small group of people on the concrete platform but saw no one familiar.

The waiting room was deserted. Matthew stepped inside. The station was cramped and old, its few leather-padded benches well worn. He sat his carpet-bag on the floor and settled on a bench to wait.

In a few moments the double doors banged open and a chattering crowd swirled in from the platform and bustled through the station. The street door slammed shut behind them.

The station was silent again, but Matthew sensed he wasn't alone. He turned toward the double doors. Framed in the doorway was the Reverend Mr. Andrew Hobson.

Matthew sprang to his feet. He started to reach down to pick up his carpetbag but stopped himself midway. He straightened and walked over to the platform doors.

The Reverend Mr. Hobson, a distinguished man a head taller than Matthew, extended his hand formally.

"It's good to see you home," he said without emotion.

"It's nice to be home, sir," Matthew replied, not meeting his father's eyes as he shook his father's hand.

The Reverend Mr. Hobson seemed to be a bit embarrassed by even this restrained contact. He dropped Matthew's hand and reached for his pocket watch.

"Come along, now," he intoned. "It's only an hour until the Sabbath." He turned abruptly and walked toward the street door.

Matthew scrambled after him, catching up his carpetbag as he passed.

His father said nothing else until they were seated in the buggy. Then the Reverend Mr. Hobson asked the dreaded question. "How are your studies progressing?"

Matthew gave the ritual answer. "I'm doing my best, sir."

"That is to be expected," came the ritual reply as his father clucked up the team and pulled away.

Matthew looked at the darkening sky. Less than an hour until sundown, he thought.

Since his childhood, the Sabbath had been both a glorious holy mystery and a terrible burden for Matthew. His father, a conservative Methodist preacher, held to the Sabbath of medieval tradition, observed from sundown Saturday until sundown Sunday.

It was taught by Matthew's father and his father's church that no work should be performed on the Sabbath. This meant that the animals were given feed enough for two days. The horses were comfortably stabled before sundown; everyone walked. No hot food could be prepared, so all the cooking for the entire weekend was done on Friday.

Children were expected to sit quietly and read their Bibles, not run or play outside. Matthew could still picture the pair of hard wooden stools beside the parlor fireplace where he and Zack had sat memorizing their church school verses. He could see every board in the floor, every flower in the parlor wallpaper, every fold in the heavy drapes.

The memory of the parsonage was so clear in Matthew's mind that he was nearly startled to look up and see the actual building before him. The Hobson family home was a large white wooden Victorian structure, set close beside the formidable stone church.

The house, built to his father's meticulous specifications, had a pillared porch and big windows facing the street. Twin attic towers rose at each end of the building. Electric lights glowed amber through lace parlor curtains.

As a child Matthew had daydreamed the towers were medieval castles; he was the knight errant who would storm them in the name of chivalry. Now he saw the house for what it was, and as he climbed down from the buggy, he wondered at the mixed physical reactions he was having: a warm glow of homecoming in his chest and a tightening knot of tension in his stomach.

In the late afternoon the church and house were pale. Beyond the church Matthew could see light streaming through the open doors of Parkman's

Livery Stable. Inside, men were sweeping the barn floor and hauling in fresh bales of hay.

Matthew nodded toward the barn. "Still having dances on Saturday nights over there?" he asked his father.

"Heathens," his father spat.

Matthew got out of the buggy and retrieved his carpetbag from the boot. His father unhitched the horses and wordlessly led them around behind the house, leaving Matthew standing alone.

Matthew stopped a moment to look down the deserted length of the porch at the empty summer rockers and picking baskets piled under the eaves. It was all exactly as he remembered it. He paused at the threshold, took a deep breath, and went inside.

Matthew set his bag down beside the hall tree in the entryway and walked quietly to the dining room. His mother was setting the table for supper, but when she looked up and saw him in the doorway, she rushed to hug him. Moments later his two sisters joined the huddle, giggling and jumping up and down, shouting, "Matthew's home! Matthew's home!"

Mary Margaret, who with great importance would tell visitors that she was eight years old, was born when the Reverend Mr. Hobson was fifty. Her sister,

Amy, arrived two years later. Their father, proper Victorian that he was, adored them while at the same time being embarrassed by this evidence of his carnal nature. The result was that he was even more strict with his daughters than he had been with his sons.

Matthew, on the other hand, doted on his little sisters and spoiled them shamelessly.

"Hello, ladies! You're really growing up," he said as he reached into his pocket and pulled out bright silk scarves for each of them. "Here—all the way from Paris. The latest thing, I'm told."

The girls squealed with delight. Matthew drew another scarf from his pocket and kissed his mother on the cheek as he gave it to her.

"You don't think it's too gay?" she asked him.

"It's what all the fashionable women are wearing," he assured her. She wrapped the scarf around her shoulders and smiled to herself.

"Matthew's home! Matthew's home!" the girls were chanting as they held hands and danced around the dining table.

The Reverend Mr. Hobson appeared in the doorway on the far side of the room.

The girls froze. Mary Margaret stuffed her scarf into her pinafore pocket. Matthew's mother stepped back, as if caught in an illicit act.

The Reverend Mr. Hobson looked sternly at the girls.

"It's five-thirty. Are your Bible lessons prepared, girls?"

Amy and Mary Margaret scurried out of the room. Matthew knew they went to the parlor bookcase and got down their small Bibles, then sat on the benches at the fireplace and piously started to memorize.

"I'm sure your mother would appreciate your help in readying the meal so she won't have to work on the Sabbath," the Reverend Mr. Hobson said to Matthew. His eyes scanned his family. "I'll be a few minutes yet in preparing my sermon for tonight. Quiet contemplation from all of you will be of great assistance to me."

Matthew went to the table and helped set out the plates. The Reverend Mr. Hobson watched impassionately. Then, satisfied, he returned to his study.

Mrs. Hobson did not look up from her task as he left. But when she was sure she had heard the door close, she said, "There's been a note from Zachary. He's built up quite a place in Colorado."

"I know," Matthew said, casting a furtive look toward the study. "He stopped by to see me at school."

Matthew and his mother exchanged looks, each trying to read the other's thoughts. After a moment she patted his hand and went toward the kitchen.

"Help me get this roast out of the oven. It's nearly time for church."

Matthew followed her into the kitchen.

Elizabeth Gregg Hobson was born the youngest of six children. Her three older brothers spoiled her; her two older sisters treated her as if she was one of their dolls, dressing her in their finest hand-me-downs and holding tea parties in her honor.

Although she was pampered as a child, Elizabeth's adulthood began suddenly and traumatically. Her mother, a hardworking Quaker who always found time to do for others but never for herself, contracted smallpox while Elizabeth was in her last year away at school. By the time Elizabeth had rushed home, her mother was dead.

Elizabeth's father, a hardheaded Methodist with whom she shared an unspoken mutual adoration, was thrown from a horse three months later. The accident left his right arm mangled and his spirit crushed. Elizabeth stayed at home and ran his household. She cooked his food, kept his house, and tried to lift his spirits.

She'd met Andrew Hobson that last year she'd lived in her father's house. Pleasantries at church functions and an occasional handshake at the church door were all that passed between Elizabeth and the new minister during the first year that they knew each other. As Elizabeth's father deteriorated, he became more and more dependent on her; Sunday morning was the only time she left his side.

Andrew respected her wishes and saw her during the week only when he made an official "family call" to her home. But as the year wore on, the family calls became more frequent. And, although the proprieties were strictly observed, Andrew and Elizabeth both felt an unspoken understanding.

Elizabeth's father died at the end of the winter. For the first year after her mother's death, Elizabeth had swathed herself in somber clothing: dark gray, deep brown, and black. But she did not resume her mourning after her father's death. She felt that he had died with her mother, with only his body lingering unhappily until he joined her.

Andrew's father and grandfathers had been ministers back as far as the family history was known. He offered a sedate life. His ways were conservative and straightforward; he needed a wife who could shoulder the considerable burdens of leading the women's auxiliaries, lend a feminine sympathy to his family calls, and keep his household running smoothly and graciously. Elizabeth evidenced all these qualities and more, and he set out to win her.

But Andrew Hobson did not sweep Elizabeth off

her feet. He appealed to her sense and logic. After all, he was not offering passion and abandon; he needed a partner in his life and his ministry, someone willing to work as hard as he to serve his church.

Elizabeth, whose adult life had been spent in service to the head of her household, found this request natural and fitting. She had no illusions about romantic love. She respected Andrew and found his lifestyle comfortable and comforting.

They married at Christmastime, before the altar of his own first church.

Elizabeth had never tried to imagine where she would be living or what she would be doing if she had chosen another path. Her life since had been rewarding spiritually, if not always emotionally. She had good, strong children; her husband was successful and content in his work. She had friends around her, respect from her community, and a home to care for.

It was enough.

Most of the congregation was already seated for evening services when the Hobson family entered the church through a side door from the parsonage garden. Every pew except the front one was full.

As was their custom, Matthew offered his mother his arm, and Mary Margaret held Amy's hand as they all filed into the front row.

Matthew glanced around the sanctuary, comfortable in the familiar surroundings. The architecture of the First Methodist Church reflected the personality of its parson: practical without style, impressive without elegance. Its hardwood floors had been burnished to a satin glow by the devoted hands of several generations of congregation ladies. The pews were made of quality wood with no flourishes. The stained-glass windows were resplendent with violent scenes of Old Testament sin and punishment.

Matthew could remember sitting awestruck in this front pew, one of several hundred faces held spellbound by his father's words. When Matthew was little, he'd thought his father was actually God, making no distinction between the disembodied deity his father preached about and the man who was absolute ruler of his own life. He was nearly ten before he was able to completely separate the Father, the Son, and the Holy Ghost of his father's invocation from his images of the man in the pulpit.

The robed choir filed in from the side chancel and took their places, singing a processional hymn as they walked. The congregation stood and sang with them.

As they sang the last verse, the Reverend Mr. Hobson entered from a door hidden behind the altar, appearing in the pulpit almost as if by magic just as the choir finished.

"Thank you, Brother Willows," he said quietly, nodding to the choir director. "Your music was, as always, inspirational."

The choir director blushed with pleasure as he motioned for the choir to be seated.

The Reverend Mr. Hobson pulled himself up to his full height, his already imposing figure made even taller by the high pulpit. He looked down upon his flock, milking the moment.

"Are you saved?" he suddenly shouted.

Several in the congregation started in their seats. A baby cried near the back of the church.

"Are you going to heaven, Brother John Davis?" the preacher asked, fixing his gaze on a well-dressed man in the fourth pew.

Brother Davis looked up, confused.

"It is easier for a camel to go through the eye of a needle than for a rich man to enter into the kingdom of God," the preacher shouted.

Brother Davis, one of the town's leading bankers, squirmed uncomfortably as the attention of the whole congregation was fixed on him.

The Reverend Mr. Hobson scanned the church for another sinner.

"How about you, Sister Mary Palmer? Have you done the Lord's work this week past?"

Sister Palmer looked stricken.

"And you, Brother William Harrington? And you, Brother Matthew Harris?"

The preacher paused for effect.

"We have all—all—fallen short in the Lord's sight this week. God knows," he intoned. "God knows."

A chorus of muttered *Amen*s rose from the congregation.

"And if we don't confess and repent our sins, the strong hand of the Lord will visit his wrath on us in the fullness of time."

Many in the congregation were now nodding in agreement. A few were murmuring "Amen" and "Praise the Lord," falling into the rhythm of the sermon.

"And those who turn away from the will of God, those will be swept clean from His firmament. Those will be cast down to the lair of Him Who Rules in Darkness."

A chorus of *Amen*s rose from the congregation.

"Satan is here in this place. In this town. Even here in the Lord's house. Some of you have invited him in, in your hearts."

Now the murmur in the church was louder, the worshipers lulled by the hypnotic voice of the preacher.

"Repent, sinners!" the preacher shouted.

A woman in the back shouted, "Hallelujah!"

"Repent, before Satan drags you down."

The crowd responded. "Yes, Jesus!" "Amen!" "Hallelujah!" The church came alive with muttered prayers.

"Repent! Satan wants to pull you down from the path of righteousness! He's out there!" the preacher shouted, pointing at the open church doors. "Out there are the paths of the eternally lost!"

The preacher's voice could barely be heard over the responses of the congregation. But from the back of the church, high and melodic over the *Amen*s and *Hallelujah*s, came a lilting fiddle tune.

The Reverend Mr. Hobson paused, listening. For a second the worshipers continued their responses, caught up in the rhythm of the sermon. Then they too stopped to listen.

"There!" cried the preacher. "Satan calls the ungodly to dance to his tune!"

The fiddle was getting louder, playing a lively jig. The fiddler made up in enthusiasm what he lacked in skill, and the rhythm was at counterpoint to the hypnotic beat of the preacher's sermon. In the distance the parishioners could hear laughter.

"The devil is calling our young people to dance on the Sabbath today so they can dance in the fires of hell tomorrow!"

The Reverend Mr. Hobson opened the Bible on the pulpit and leafed through it, looking for a passage. He paused for emphasis, then began to read.

"Thou shalt not tempt . . ."

The fiddle changed to a reel, the music flowing rich and full.

The Reverend Mr. Hobson beat his fist on the pulpit. "By God, I'll not have it!"

He slammed the Bible shut and, tucking it under his arm, rushed down from the pulpit, up the main aisle, and out the door.

The congregation sat stunned for a second. Then, as one body, they rose from the seats and streamed out the door after their preacher.

In the front pew Matthew's mother turned to him, not daring to rise on her own. Matthew shrugged. "Well, we may as well go watch," he said.

His mother sat, gathering her poise. "It isn't seemly," she said softly, pulling the two little girls back into their seats.

Matthew headed for the door.

The Reverend Mr. Hobson flung the side door of the livery stable open with enough force to send it slamming back against the side of the barn.

"Stop!" he shouted. "Stop this minute!" He stood in the doorway, glowering.

A score of couples in the center of the barn stopped and turned toward the door, still paired for the reel the fiddler had been playing. The big barn had been swept clean; the horses were corralled outside, and the barn was decked out for a party, with streamers and bunting strung in the rafters and along the loft. Tables had been set up along the walls to form a makeshift sideboard bent with the weight of the food from the picnic baskets stowed underneath.

The scruffy fiddler sat at the other end of the barn, where a bandstand had been improvised out of hay bales. He put his fiddle aside and grinned as the Reverend Mr. Hobson strode the length of the barn up to the bandstand.

"In the name of God, repent your sin and stop this blasphemy," the preacher commanded, his voice edged with steel.

The itinerant fiddler leaned back against a hay bale and settled in. He'd heard it all before. "Now, Preacher, don't get your back up," the fiddler said. "Folks here just steppin' out a bit."

The preacher shook the Bible in the fiddler's face. "Stepping away from the paths of righteousness, you mean. I'll not have it."

The fiddler smirked. "Can't say you have any choice, Preacher. These folks just came here for a good time."

The Reverend Mr. Hobson raised his Bible in the air and brandished it at the crowd. "Repent of your evil and sin no more!" he shouted. The crowd moved back; one of the dancers laughed.

The preacher turned on the fiddler. "Take your instrument of evil elsewhere," he hissed.

"Now I can't rightly do that. These folks already paid me."

The preacher gestured to encompass the crowd. "These simple folk know not what they do. They are easily led astray."

A huge farmer stepped from the crowd and stood nose to nose with the preacher. "Who you calling simple?" he demanded.

The crowd murmured. The fiddler surveyed his audience, then stood and got between the preacher and the angry farmer.

"Now, Preacher, you said your piece," the fiddler said. "Maybe you better get on back to your congregation and let us get on with our music. I think you've taken about enough of these good folks' time."

The dancers muttered their assent. "Yeah, get him outta here," the big farmer grumbled.

The fiddler struck up "Fiddler's Joy," a lively dance tune. A woman at the edge of the crowd hooked her elbow in the preacher's arm and spun him onto the dance floor. Another dancer, inspired by her boldness, joined in the impromptu do-si-do. Other dancers joined in, twirling the Reverend Mr. Hobson through the crowd, closer and closer to the barn door.

Matthew had been standing at the barn door; he had seen everything. Now as his father was roughly caromed toward the door, he slipped outside.

The Reverend Mr. Hobson was scarcely holding his balance as he was twirled across the dance floor. "God will have his way yet!" he shouted over his shoulder as a tall woman in a calico dress gave him a final twist and sent him spinning into the street.

"God—meaning him!" The woman laughed as she went back to her partner.

Five hours later the barn dance was over, and the fiddler was packing his instrument into a battered wooden case when he felt the presence of someone behind him. He spun around to find the Reverend Mr. Hobson standing at the edge of the bandstand.

"Didn't get enough a while ago?" The fiddler grinned.

The preacher stepped closer and spoke quietly but firmly. "I came to ask you, in the name of God, to move on."

The fiddler seemed to consider the request. "God

ain't never cared too much about me and mine," he said. "I got three more nights to play here. Like I told you, I already been paid."

The Reverend Mr. Hobson pulled himself up to his full height and dignity, straightening his shoulders. "I will not have the good people of this parish defiled by you."

The fiddler came down from the bandstand. "Now wait just a damn minute. I give folks a little pleasure, that's all."

"Sin for money." The preacher sniffed. "How much are you paid for the Devil's work?"

"A dollar a night, if it's any business of yours."

The Reverend Mr. Hobson leaned across the bandstand and opened the fiddle case. He pulled out the fiddle and held it up to the light. The fiddler reached to retrieve it, but the preacher turned away.

"A dollar? That's three for the rest of your time." He turned and looked the fiddler in the eye. "I'll give you thirty if you'll move on."

The fiddler took the fiddle back and put it in the case. "Look," he said, "I told you. I already been paid by Mr. Parkman. In advance."

The Reverend Mr. Hobson reached for the fiddle case. "I will repay Mr. Parkman, and you can keep the additional money if you give me your word that you'll never come back here again. But you must throw in your fiddle, here, to assure me that you'll move on tonight."

"But how am I gonna make a living without my fiddle?"

"How much is a new one?" the preacher asked.

The fiddler thought for a moment. "Maybe three dollars up in Chicago."

The Reverend Mr. Hobson reached into his pocket and pulled out three ten-dollar gold pieces. He handed them to the fiddler. "Then I suggest you proceed to Chicago posthaste with the profits from this transaction."

The fiddler pocketed the money and handed over the fiddle, saying, "Well, I'll be damned."

"Quite possibly," the preacher said, tucking the case under his arm and stalking from the room.

Matthew's childhood bedroom always felt odd when he came home now, an unsettling mixture of the strange and the familiar. He remembered the wallpaper brighter, the furniture newer, the rugs softer on his bare feet.

His memories of the room were from the eye level of a younger boy, and he was always surprised at how diminutive the furnishings seemed. As he prepared for bed, Matthew realized that the tall dressing table that he had once had to stand on tiptoe to reach now barely came up to his waist. With a smile, he noticed he was bending over to see himself in the mirror.

He got into bed and pulled the familiar quilt up around him. The bed seemed a bit too close to the ground, but it was his own bed; he could feel the spot on the headboard where he had tried out the pocket-knife he got when he was ten. The ceiling that had once appeared to be as tall as the trees seemed lower now, but he could still see the indentation in the corner made by his first slingshot. His eyes wandered around the room, picking out reassuring landmarks of his boyhood as he lay awake in the dark.

The preacher entered the parsonage yard by the back gate, the fiddle case under his arm. The yard was small, dominated by a lone maple tree. The moonlight washed the scene sea green, bright enough that he could see the shadowy mass of several cords of firewood piled high beside the porch steps.

He walked along the path toward the back door of the parsonage.

The Reverend Mr. Hobson stepped up onto the porch; then, apparently thinking better of it, he turned to the woodpile. With a mighty heave he threw the fiddle case on top of the stacked wood.

The case clattered across the split wood and flipped over. The small brass catch gave way, spilling the fiddle out onto the rough wood. It came to rest upside down, partially hidden in the stack.

Without looking back, the preacher went inside.

Matthew, drawn to his window by the click of the back-gate latch, came closer to the pane. He waited until he heard the solid *chunk* as the door to his parents' bedroom closed.

As Matthew came down by the back stairs, a light drizzle began to fall.

The back door of the parsonage opened noiselessly as Matthew slipped out onto the porch. He was barefoot, only a flimsy robe over his nightshirt.

He crept down the steps into the yard. Hardly daring to breathe, he stretched to reach the fiddle on the woodpile. A split log skittered across the pile; Matthew's eyes quickly darted to the upstairs bedroom window where his parents slept, but no light came on.

He stood on tiptoe in his bare feet, and this time his fingertips touched the fiddle. It rotated in place.

The slim neck of the fiddle moved toward him. He grasped it and pulled.

The fiddle case was easier, and he got it on the first try. Matthew stroked the wooden side of the fiddle, then rubbed his hand across the strings. The fiddle resonated softly as Matthew put it into the case and snapped shut the brass catch.

He looked up furtively at his parents' window. The curtains were still drawn, the windows dark. He put the fiddle case under his arm as he stole back into the house.

It was night; of that Matthew was sure, but he could not have said if he was awake or asleep. He heard a noise at the side of the bed. He rolled over and saw his mother standing beside him, finger to her lips to quiet him.

"It's good to have you home," she whispered.

He noticed the scent of her rose toilet water as she kissed him gently on the forehead. He started to say something, to sit up in bed and hug her, but she swirled noiselessly out of the room.

The next thing he knew, it was morning.

CHAPTER

Nebraska is cold in January.

That is the fact, but beyond fact is the wet, bone-aching cold that permeates the body and chills the soul. The world becomes flat, line-of-sight horizontal in the plane of the wind. It is too cold to look up and see the glazed sky.

The trees stood defenseless and naked, while under them the students bundled futilely as they scurried between heated buildings.

Matthew, driven indoors, was bored. His mind would not absorb another Bible verse or geometry formula. During the first two weeks after his return to school, he had read the novels his brother had sent him, and the college library had only religious materials and reference texts.

Then he remembered the fiddle. He retrieved it

from under the bed and pulled a few scratchy sounds—not quite notes—from the old instrument.

Matthew grimaced. It sure didn't sound the way it had when the fiddler played it.

He tried again, this time holding the bow more firmly. A crisp note emerged, disintegrating into cat squalls at the end.

Better, he thought—but not much.

But by the end of the afternoon he could scratch out a simple tune, and his boredom had lifted. When he went down to supper, he felt refreshed for the first time in a long while.

The cold and wind imprisoned Matthew indoors, away from his emancipating walks in the countryside. Classes would not start for another week, and he turned more and more to the fiddle for solace.

Matthew's self-taught technique was still awful, but the fiddle felt right; it was good in his hand. He loved to run his fingers over the polished wood. The strings sang gently when he ran his fingertips across them.

And there was a thrill that Matthew would not have admitted to anyone, even to Cappy, the first time he coaxed a clear tone from the instrument. He stroked the bow firmly across the strings, and the fiddle responded to his touch, the smoky undertones mixing with a high, sweet tenor note. Matthew yelled with excitement, then looked around sheepishly to be sure no one had heard.

His success bred a desire for more, and he practiced most of his waking hours. The fiddle was no longer a trophy, an acquisition secreted from his father. He had claimed it.

Matthew had the fiddle in his hand when he heard Cappy's key in the lock. He hid it behind his back and kicked the fiddle case under the bed just as Cappy came in, balancing his suitcases and tennis racket.

"Well, the prodigal returns," Cappy quipped. "When did you get back?"

"Very funny," Matthew retorted. "Almost three weeks ago."

"What's that?" Cappy asked, peering behind Matthew.

"What's what?"

"That," Cappy said, pointing at the edge of the fiddle peeking out from behind Matthew.

"Mine," said Matthew firmly, a bit embarrassed.

Cappy threw his hands up into the air. "OK, don't get your back up."

As Cappy turned away to put his suitcase in the closet, Matthew slid the fiddle under the bed.

"I'm going over to the gym. Some of the fellows are

stringing a tennis net. Want to come?" Cappy asked.

"It's snowing!" Matthew laughed. "Tennis season is over."

Cappy grinned. "Or just beginning."

Matthew shook his head. "Think I'll stay here and hit the books. Classes start Monday, you know."

"All work and no play—" Cappy began.

"Keeps me in school another day," Matthew finished for him.

"Suit yourself." Cappy shrugged. He put on his tennis togs, then bundled his coat and scarf over them.

"You look ridiculous," Matthew commented.

"You are a gentleman and a scholar." Cappy winked as he picked up his racket and left.

Matthew sat at the desk and dug out his textbooks. After a few minutes' review he realized how far behind he was; much of the material made little or no sense to him. The frustration came rushing back: the futility of scrambling for information he couldn't see any use for, to attain a future he wasn't sure he wanted anymore.

He got his folder of lessons, hoping to see a direction in which to begin to study. Perhaps if he could use them to review, he might at least make it through his term finals.

Matthew studied the first geometry paper and wrote

the answer to a problem in the margin. He checked his answer against the answer in the textbook and shook his head. He refigured the formula. He still didn't see how the answer in the textbook was derived.

Well, maybe it was just that particular problem. He pulled out a second lesson sheet and calculated the answer to another problem. He checked the book and once again reworked the problem.

When he checked the answer, it was wrong.

"I just don't see . . ." he said to himself.

Matthew studied the book for a few more seconds, then slammed it shut. He retrieved his fiddle and began to play.

A few days later Cappy was climbing the dorm stairs when he heard fiddle music coming from the room. He stood outside and listened a few minutes, then burst inside.

Matthew guiltily thrust the fiddle under his pillow.

"What's that you've got under the pillow?" Cappy prodded. "It's too small to be a girl."

Matthew sheepishly held out the fiddle.

"Is *that* what all the mystery's been about?" Cappy teased.

Matthew was angry now. "What right do you have to tell me what I can do in my own room? You sure think you have the right to clutter up everything with your tennis junk."

Cappy snickered. "I don't care if you play it naked in the middle of the quadrangle! I just think it's funny, that's all. I thought there was some deep, dark secret, dirty pictures or something."

Matthew felt invaded. "It's just private, *that's* all."

"I don't give a damn if you want to saw away on that thing," Cappy said. "Just keep the noise down. It sounds like you're killing a cat."

"I'm getting better," Matthew said defensively.

"You couldn't get worse," Cappy said as Matthew placed the fiddle carefully in its case.

At 4 A.M., the college town was silent outside Matthew's window. But he lay awake, listening, waiting for some sound on which to focus instead of the jumble in his mind: a snatch of an essay he was writing; his father's face; a fragment of a geometry equation; a bit of Bible verse; his mother's voice, then his father preaching—and then himself, a decade older, standing stiffly at his own pulpit; a chemistry formula, perhaps right, perhaps wrong; Zack's bull, Adonis. He grasped at the images, trying to find the one that was important, but they swirled past him at equal volume and were gone.

Outside, a mockingbird anticipating the dawn began its song, trilling a quartet of notes over and over. The fiddler's tune entwined itself with the bird's melody in Matthew's mind. He released himself back into restless sleep, his left hand twitching the violin fingering.

Dr. Percy Tillinghast delivered his theology lectures as if his words were themselves Holy Writ. Matthew found the hours he was forced to spend in the huge amphitheater interminable.

The lecturer stood at the blackboard at the bottom of a dozen steep concentric tiers of desks: The Pit. Matthew always sat at the far wall on the highest semicircle so as to be less subject to the professor's glance or, God forbid, chance question. Dr. Tillinghast's pompous monotone was difficult to understand at that distance, but Matthew always took frantic, copious notes.

Dr. Tillinghast had collected up everyone's theme books and graded them three days before finals. Matthew watched as the stacks of books were passed along the rows, then handed up to the next tier and passed along again.

"I suggest you take these grades to heart," Dr. Tillinghast was saying. "I was not at all pleased with the performance of the class as a whole."

The students were murmuring among themselves, opening their theme books and shaking their heads.

"It will be necessary for you to apply yourselves for the rest of the term if you plan to succeed in this class, and in your chosen vocations," Dr. Tillinghast said, his tone smug.

The stack was in Matthew's row now. Finally the last two theme books came to the boy sitting next to him. The boy opened both books, grinned, and handed Matthew's across.

Matthew opened the cover of the theme book and glanced quickly at the grade.

A large *F* was marked in red ink.

Matthew tilted his head back and closed his eyes in despair, no longer listening to the lecturer.

Later that evening Matthew sat at his desk, as usual hopelessly lost in a geometry problem.

After scratching through the answer for the fourth time, he sought refuge in the fiddle, the sweet music emerging from his hand as if the instrument played itself.

But for once there was no solace here. The music seemed to Matthew stilted and cold, not soothing but strident.

After a while he put the fiddle away and went back to his desk, finally admitting what must be done. Setting his schoolwork aside, he took out a sheet of Cappy's writing paper and began to write.

Father:

Although I have applied myself this term as you asked, I still do not seem to grasp the work my professors are giving me.

Matthew hesitated with his pen, crafting the words carefully. The fiddle case rested against the leg of his chair, and he stroked it absently for courage before he wrote again.

If you would allow it, I would like to come home when this term ends. I believe my distraction may be in part due to my confusion about my future, and I want to talk with you about whether I really have a calling to preach.

I hope you can forgive the disappointment I have caused you. I have tried my best.

Your loving son, Matthew

The Reverend Mr. Hobson stood next to his blazing fireplace six mornings later, reading the letter from his son. His face showed no emotion.

He fingered the single sheet of inexpensive paper—

not the elegant bond he had given his son to take to college. He read the letter again, more carefully this time, then carried it to his desk and laid it on the blotter. He seated himself and took out pen and paper.

He sat for a few seconds, poised over the blank sheet.

After a few more moments he put the paper back into its sheaf and carefully placed the pen back in its silver tray.

With dignity the preacher stood and carried the letter to the fireplace and let the sheet slip from his hand. It fluttered gently in the updraft before settling on to the flames.

Matthew was sitting in the uppermost row of the amphitheater, frantically scribbling notes as Dr. Tillinghast droned his first theology lecture of the new term, when the messenger came. The side door of the hall swung open noiselessly and Matthew's fate—in the person of Dayton Nichols, the dean's clerk and a sometime tennis partner of Cappy's—came in.

Nichols handed the note to Dr. Tillinghast.

"Matthew Hobson to Dean Anders's office," Dr. Tillinghast announced perfunctorily.

"Here, sir," Matthew responded as he stood.

"Go quietly," Dr. Tillinghast said, turning back to his lecture notes. Nichols shot Matthew a knowing glance as Matthew gathered his books and followed him, ignoring the snide whispered remarks that pursued them out the door.

Matthew knocked timidly on Dean Anders's door.

"Come," was the muffled response from inside.

"Take a seat, Mr. Hobson," the dean said, motioning to the huge leather chair in front of the desk.

Matthew sat as if he was being strapped into the electric chair. The huge chair enfolded him.

Dean Anders fixed him with a clinical eye.

"You are aware of the reason for this interview?"

Matthew nodded, too miserable to speak.

"Your grades, Mr. Hobson," Dean Anders said, leaning intimidatingly on his desk. "Your grades are altogether unsatisfactory. You do realize that, Mr. Hobson?"

"Yes, sir." Matthew nodded.

"This is not the first time we've spoken about this subject, is it, Mr. Hobson? I think we've discussed it at length, and you promised to redeem yourself. Is that not the case?"

"Yes, and I've tried to . . ."

"What you have tried to do and what you have accomplished seem to be two different matters, Mr. Hobson."

The dean shuffled through a file on his desk. "Just

look at these grades, Mr. Hobson. Bible history, *D*-minus. Theology, an *F*."

Dean Anders shook the paper at Matthew. "How can you possibly hope to be a minister with such grades in crucial subjects?"

Matthew shrugged, not daring to meet the dean's eyes.

"You have disgraced yourself and the hopes your father had for you," the dean said.

He stopped to appraise Matthew sternly.

"It is the assessment of your teachers that you have no aptitude for this work, and that you would be better off to pursue some other vocation."

The dean paused for a moment, then glared at Matthew. "I share that assessment."

Matthew blanched. "But, sir, I've been trying to . . ."

The dean waved him away. "I'm afraid it's no longer enough. You are no longer able to meet the minimum qualifications for enrollment at this college. You will be dropped from the student roster at once."

Matthew was frantic. "But, sir, my father . . ."

The dean shrugged his shoulders; he had washed his hands of the problem. "I've written to inform your father to expect you home by the end of the week, and the reason for your return."

The dean seemed to have ended the interview, but Matthew couldn't move. He was wounded, cornered, a small helpless animal beaten into submission.

The dean saw the defeat in the boy's eyes, and only then did he soften his tone slightly.

"I'm sorry, but this may be for the best. Your true vocation may lie elsewhere. Give yourself the opportunity to find it."

"But my father wants . . ." Matthew began helplessly.

Dean Anders's face hardened. "It is rather too late to consider what your father wants. Please make formal withdrawal through the admissions office as you leave campus."

"Yes, sir," Matthew replied automatically. The boy sat, staring at his hands.

"That will be all, Mr. Hobson."

"Yes, sir," Matthew said, lifting the suddenly enormous weight of his body from the chair.

Matthew walked to the door as if moving underwater. As he opened the door, he turned to the dean.

"Thank you, sir," he said.

Cappy was lying on his bed reading a dime novel when Matthew burst through the doorway. Matthew went straight to the closet and wrestled his trunk into the center of the room. He threw his books on the bed and started pitching clothes into the trunk.

This was finally enough to rouse Cappy from his book.

"What the hell are you doing?" he demanded, tossing the novel aside and standing up to be out of the line of fire.

"What does it look like? I've been expelled."

"Jesus," Cappy exhaled.

"Chessboard mine or yours?" Matthew asked, nodding to the ongoing game on the table between their beds.

"Board's yours, pieces are mine," Cappy said, scrambling to stay out of the way.

Matthew reached for the chessboard. He swept the chess pieces off with his arm, scattering them across the room, and folded the board into his trunk.

"Checkmate," he said grimly.

He looked up, fixing Cappy's eyes with his own. "I never belonged here in the first place."

Cappy sat on the far side of his bed, watching Matthew pack. Matthew worked his way around the room, throwing shirts and trousers haphazardly at the trunk from across the room.

Matthew's skin prickled with the sensation that a steel brush was scouring his arms and legs. He picked up a history assignment from the desk, wanting something real in his hands, something solid and familiar. But the words on the page seemed scrambled; the letters were recognizable, but the combinations made no sense.

Matthew tore the paper in half. He scooped up the other loose papers on his desktop and threw them all in the trash can.

In a burst of manic energy he rushed around the room, frantically opening drawers and cabinets, pulling schoolbooks and papers out and throwing them away.

He grabbed a parcel of his father's letters from the bedside stand. "I guess I won't need these anymore," he said, throwing them out. "He can be disappointed with me in person from now on."

Matthew gathered his school sweaters, pennants, and other mementos and carried these to the trash can also. As he stood there beside the now-empty desk, his school life discarded, his rage grew. He grabbed the can, threw open the door, and stalked down the back stairs to throw can and contents in the dustbin.

By the time he'd climbed the stairs back to his room, Matthew was seized by dawning horror.

There it finally was: He was expelled. His worst nightmare had congealed as fact, into the fury he would face from his father when the expulsion was known. The terror had become real. Finally, exhausted, he sat on his bed.

"What am I going to say to my father?" he asked, more to himself than to Cappy.

"Tell him you did the best you could," Cappy said softly.

Matthew smiled a wry little smile.

"So what are you going to do now, Preacher?" Cappy asked, trying to keep his tone light.

"Don't call me that!" Matthew snapped. Then, seeing Cappy's chastised expression, he softened his tone. "I don't know," he said quietly as he sat on the edge of the bed. "I can't even think about it."

"Well, it's not the end of the world. You'll feel better once you get home."

To Matthew, the walls and ceiling of the room telescoped in. He could make no sense of it. The flowers in the wallpaper blended together into a potpourri more vivid than any colors he had ever known before.

Cappy went to the desk and started sorting the papers in the drawers. "I'll help you get this tangle sorted out," he said. "I'll dump the lessons, but you have some letters and personal things in this mess. I'll just make stacks."

Matthew no longer heard Cappy's voice; instead a low humming in his ears had begun to grow louder. He vaguely perceived that Cappy's lips still moved, but the humming drowned out the sound. He had no knowledge that the humming came from his own throat.

Cappy reached under the bed and retrieved Matthew's fiddle case and sat it on the bed. Matthew drew the case across his lap. He took the fiddle out, running his fingers lightly over the bow.

At the desk Cappy was still working away. "If you don't want to take all your things now, I'll put them down in the basement for you until you get settled."

Matthew set the bow on the bed, and holding the fiddle like a guitar, began to softly pluck an old-time hymn, a favorite of his mother's.

Cappy worked on. "If you want to, maybe you can come out to my parents' house at the holidays. Your dad might make it rough for you if you stay there, but if you come out, we could have some fun. We could get some skates and skate on the river. . . ."

Matthew shuddered, chilled. "I feel all prickly," he whispered. He picked up the bow and began to play the hymn.

Cappy finished sorting the debris on the desk. "OK, this pile on the chair is all yours."

Matthew was deeply absorbed in his music, playing technically well but without emotion.

"What do you want me to do with it?" Cappy asked.

Matthew closed his eyes.

"Matt?"

Cappy saw that Matthew was far away.

"Fine," he said. "Get it out of your system. I'll bring you back a sandwich."

Cappy grabbed his jacket and left for the student union to get their lunch.

Forty-five minutes later Cappy reentered the dorm lobby juggling a pile of sandwiches and hot coffee in a ceramic carafe. He climbed the stairs to their room. From the landing he could hear that Matthew was still sawing away on the fiddle. The tune was the same hymn he had been playing when Cappy left.

"Hey, sport, you're in a rut," he joked as he came in. "Don't you know any dance tunes?"

Matthew sat on the edge of the bed with his back to the door, his position unchanged from the moment Cappy had left.

Cappy put the food down on the desk and walked over to Matthew. "Matt?"

Matthew did not respond. The lifeless hymn droned on.

Cappy shook him by the shoulder. "Matthew, what is it?"

The fiddle fell from Matthew's hands and clattered

to the floor. Matthew was crying without sound, without movement.

"Jesus, Matthew!" Cappy exclaimed in shock.

Matthew stared straight ahead, not responding as Cappy called to him and shook him.

"Matt! Matthew!"

Cappy flung the door open. "Mrs. McWorthy!" Cappy yelled, but there was no answer.

"Get Dr. Swanson, quick!" he shouted at a passing student. The kid took one look at Cappy's face and ran.

Ten minutes later Dr. Swanson was bending over Matthew. He passed his hand in front of Matthew's unfocused eyes.

"Recent illnesses? Sudden shocks?" he asked Cappy.

"He just got expelled," Cappy responded.

The doctor shook his head in sympathy.

"That would do it," the doctor ventured. "Exhaustion, I'd say. This boy's had a hard time of it."

"That's the gospel truth," Cappy said.

The doctor tucked Matthew into the bed, then turned to Cappy.

"This is more than we can deal with at the infirmary," Dr. Swanson said gravely. The college had no facilities to care for a seriously ill student. Most medical emergencies were handled by the local hospital, but it would not admit psychiatric patients.

"Can you stay with him while I make some arrangements?" he asked Cappy.

"Sure," said Cappy, glancing at Matthew's quiet form. "Say, he's not going to . . . do anything, is he?"

The doctor looked again at Matthew. "No, I doubt he will even move. He's a very sick boy."

The doctor glanced around the room. "Get his things together, will you? He won't be coming back."

"Can he take his fiddle?" Cappy asked.

"Too dangerous to let him have those strings right now," the doctor answered. Then, seeing Cappy's shocked face, he gentled his voice a bit. "He won't be playing it for a while anyway," the doctor said. "You keep it for him."

While Cappy warily waited upstairs with Matthew, Dr. Swanson telephoned the state asylum. The waiting list was four months long, he was told—and then there was no possibility of admitting Matthew without formal commitment.

And so he tried Dr. Oscar Milton, a medical school colleague who ran a private asylum called Milton's Rest on the outskirts of the town. Dr. Milton had, with two partners, founded the sanitarium twenty years earlier as a refuge for well-to-do patients, and as a steady source of income for themselves. As superintendent and an owner of the asylum, Dr. Milton tolerated no interference in the operations of his hospital or in its cash flow.

Was there a means of support for the boy? Dr. Milton inquired early in the conversation.

Dr. Swanson had to admit that, for the moment, there was not.

"Ah, well," Dr. Milton said. "We'll make some arrangement until the boy's father can arrive. We'll have the police transport him, in case he turns out to be a danger. Let me know when the father is in touch, will you?"

Just before sunset two large police officers arrived. Matthew walked quietly between them, leaning heavily against first one, then the other. He never spoke.

Dr. Swanson and Cappy trailed behind. But when they reached the street, the cops stopped Cappy and the doctor from boarding the wagon. "Dr. Milton said just the boy," the taller of the cops said. "Less likely to cause trouble if he's by himself."

Cappy started to object, but Dr. Swanson put his arm around Cappy's shoulder. "Milton's the best," he said. "I suppose he knows what needs to be done. I'll go out and see Matthew tomorrow."

Later that night Dr. Swanson sent a cable to the parsonage at Brookbend.

Packing Matthew's things helped Cappy a little to deal with his friend's collapse. Though sloppy with his own clothes, Cappy carefully folded Matthew's shirts and pants. Matthew's ties, usually draped with Cappy's over a brass ring on the wall, were folded neatly over cardboard and fit flat into a drawer in the trunk. The fiddle went with Matthew's tennis racket and chessboard into the steamer trunk's roomy wardrobe.

Cappy put the trunk in storage in the basement of the dorm building—no one would come looking for Matthew's belongings very soon. It looked as if Matthew was going to be gone for a long, long time.

CHAPTER

Matthew paid little attention to his new quarters: a cell that measured six feet by eight feet, with a cot, blanket, and slop pail. He was preoccupied with The Gentleman.

Matthew had glimpsed him only once. He saw, through the barred window of his cell, an elegantly dressed man. The man casually glanced down at Matthew and seemed to smile. Through the interminable morning Matthew became sure that the man had been employed to gain his confession. Who had hired him and what crime was to be confessed was unclear.

Dr. Milton gazed at Matthew through the small cell window. The boy lay crumpled at the foot of his cot, apparently unaware of his surroundings. Hospital or jail, Dr. Milton thought, this one won't know the difference. He'll be fine here until his father arrives to guarantee his treatment. The doctor tipped the guard a quarter to make sure.

No one spoke to him; Matthew was sure that this incarceration was in punishment for a crime so heinous that his jailers were unwilling to confront him with it. The bars at the windows and the uniformed guards were ample evidence to Matthew that his offense had been grave indeed.

He was convinced the guards were observing him when he was awake, and sneaking along the corridor in the dark to overhear his dreams.

Matthew remained silent.

Dr. Swanson parked under a big tree in the courtyard of the private hospital and strode up the marble steps to the reception area. The room looked more like a hotel lobby than a hospital. He gave Matthew's name.

"I'm sorry, Doctor, but we have no patient named Hobson," the receptionist said.

Dr. Milton came out of a side office. "John! What brings you out here?"

"I've come to check on Matthew Hobson," Dr. Swanson said.

"We haven't picked him up yet. Still waiting on the paperwork, I believe."

"What do you mean, you haven't picked him up? The police took him yesterday," Dr. Swanson said.

"I don't believe arrangements have been made yet for his care," Dr. Milton said in a silky voice.

"Where is he, Oscar? Where did the police take him if they didn't bring him here?" Dr. Swanson said in alarm.

"They usually hold the violent ones in custody until we can take them," Dr. Milton said.

Dr. Swanson turned on his heel and ran for the door.

Matthew was running a low-grade fever, Dr. Swanson decided, and his chest sounded full of liquid. The boy lay motionless on the cot in his cell. "He has a bad congestive cough," Dr. Swanson said, outraged, knowing the illness came from the dank air in the basement.

He asked the guards if Matthew had been eating and was told that he'd ignored all food. The guards had forced water down his throat, but they had not been inclined to force-feed him, so the boy had gone hungry.

Intolerable, the doctor thought. "I'm taking him out of here," Dr. Swanson said.

"Can't do it, buddy," a guard said. "Dr. Milton got the judge to put him in protective custody, and he's the one's got to get him out."

"We'll see," said Dr. Swanson.

Dr. Swanson drove out to Milton's Rest and demanded to see his old classmate.

"I'll pay until we can contact the boy's family," Dr. Swanson said, his jaw tight. "Get him out of that jail."

Dr. Milton smiled and pressed a button on his desk. "Go with Dr. Swanson, here, to pick up a new patient," he said to the two uniformed attendants who came in a few moments later.

Dr. Milton was waiting in his small office when Dr. Swanson led Matthew in.

"Now, Matthew, I want you to understand that your commitment here is entirely voluntary," Dr. Milton said pleasantly. "By law we are required to tell you that. And I need for you to sign this."

He produced a typed document of several pages from the stack of papers on his desk and handed it to Matthew.

Matthew tried to read the top sheet, but only fragments of the sentences formed ideas for him. The words "agree to commitment" made sense. So did "restraints and confinement at the discretion of " and "medical treatment as deemed necessary by."

But it was a sentence at the beginning of the second page which, for Matthew, clarified what the situation was. The sentence read, in part, ". . . ongoing investigation into the history and illness of . . ."

So that was it; this was his sentencing. That there had been no trial was irrelevant to the deduction. Matthew was being asked to agree to incarceration for his crimes.

Matthew experienced relief that the moment had arrived. No more waiting, no more fearful anticipation. The time for his penance had come.

He took the proffered fountain pen and signed each of the sheets where the doctor indicated. And as the last sheet was signed, he pardoned himself for the crime he believed he had committed. He no longer felt that he was being watched or investigated. Matthew's delusion dissolved, leaving only a profound confusion and sadness.

Dr. Swanson went back to his office and, hands shaking with rage, sent a second wire to the parsonage in Brookbend.

There was no reply.

The dayroom had once been white, but the wooden benches along the walls, the plaster ceiling, even the walls themselves had gone pale gray from the many layers of cheap paint. The color had been washed right out of the floor tiles over the years. Little sunlight penetrated the dust on the barred windows.

Within this colorless environment moved dozens of inmates, like the flickering images of silent films. They were seated on the benches or in mismatched chairs or just slumped on the floor. They were the very old, and young teenagers, and all ages between. They were all the same. They were the lost.

Some of the inmates moved spasmodically. Others stared off into space. A few were bound in strait-jackets. One adolescent was curled in a fetal position, alone in the open space at the center of the room.

Most subdued were those who were sane but held here just the same: the homeless men and women to whom the state had assigned a terrible home. They stayed for years or lifetimes, their will to protest passing with the seasons, while the asylum collected on the government contract at five dollars a month for each.

Here too were the drunkards who had become feeble or violent, whose families were no longer willing to hide or excuse them. Most had been dry for years, but their loved ones would not chance having them in their midst. Many lost their reason and now, madmen themselves, they stayed.

Except for the few who talked to themselves, the group as a whole was eerily quiet. A doctor had once described them by saying they were "able to walk through one another without leaving a trace."

Dr. Milton and Dr. Harrison found Matthew sitting on the floor against the wall, running his finger along the cracks in the floor tile.

Dr. Milton shuffled through a sheaf of papers on his clipboard.

"Hobson," he announced. "Yes, here. Matthew, it is. Dementia praecox."

Dr. Harrison shook his head. "I don't know," he said skeptically. "The parents didn't indicate any history."

Dr. Milton shrugged. "Let's talk to the father again."

At the mention of his father Matthew looked up, showing no emotion.

The doctors noticed his response.

"Would you like to see your father?" Dr. Milton asked pleasantly.

Matthew mumbled something. The doctors bent to hear him.

"What, Matthew?" coaxed Dr. Milton.

"I can't think," Matthew whispered to himself.

Dr. Harrison put his hand on Matthew's shoulder.

"That's why you're here—so we can help you." He moved to help the boy to his feet.

"He put a humming in my head," Matthew murmured. "There's humming."

"Who did?" asked Dr. Harrison.

Matthew shook his head, to clear it. "I can't tell you," he said firmly.

"Why not?" asked Dr. Harrison.

"I can't think about it," Matthew said.

He struggled for a moment to rise. His body shut down under him, and he sank back to the floor.

"Shall we take him in now?" Dr. Milton asked.

They helped Matthew to stand, and he shuffled off between them.

The Reverend Mr. Hobson and his wife waited in uncomfortable wooden chairs as Matthew was brought into the superintendent's office. Dr. Harrison seated Matthew opposite them; the boy sat silently in his chair, uncomprehending and blinking in the bright light.

Mrs. Hobson started to go to her son, but her husband's firm grip at her elbow stopped her. She sat back down and averted her eyes.

"He's shirking," the Reverend Mr. Hobson said, leveling his gaze on Matthew. The boy seemed to shrink in his chair.

"Sir," Dr. Swanson said softly from his chair in the corner, "I think you can see that your son is quite ill."

"I can see that he has totally abrogated his school responsibilities. Utterly irresponsible."

Dr. Milton and Dr. Harrison glanced at each other before replying.

"This is an illness," Dr. Harrison began. "Matthew is a very sick boy."

The preacher turned on his son. "Pray," he said in a low voice, his face inches from Matthew's own face. "Pray, and God will make you whole."

Matthew flinched.

"Perhaps Matthew needs—" Mrs. Hobson began.

"What Matthew needs is to pull himself together," said the Reverend Mr. Hobson, turning on his wife. "I won't coddle him."

Mrs. Hobson, totally subdued, withdrew.

The preacher turned to the doctors. "And I won't pay you to do it. That school sent him here, and the school can pay for his keep." He looked away from Matthew. "I will pray for him."

"It will take more than prayer," snapped Dr. Swanson.

The Reverend Mr. Hobson spun on him. "Not from me, it won't," he said. "And not from you either," he said, fixing his wife's eye. "Do you understand, Elizabeth?"

Mrs. Hobson was crushed. The doctors stood by, defenseless to help.

"We must stand firm in our faith," the preacher said very quietly. "It is all we have in this world."

Mrs. Hobson's face reddened, but she was silent.

Matthew started to hum softly under his breath as Dr. Harrison rose from his chair and began to speak. Matthew heard only fragments of the conversation through his humming, and to him they were unintelligible.

". . . extended treatment . . ."

Matthew saw that his mother sat motionless, averting her eyes. His father came into his line of sight, lips moving in conversation without sound.

He saw his father gesture emphatically, but the gesture was meaningless.

". . . your responsibility . . ."

Matthew saw Dr. Milton stir his coffee. The clink of the spoon was as loud as a bell. Matthew's mind juxtaposed it with the bell on his father's church, drowning the conversation as the doctor's lips moved.

The doctors and the Reverend Mr. Hobson argued, the sound jumping in and out beneath Matthew's humming.

". . . disgrace to the family . . ." his father said.

Matthew saw a magazine on Dr. Milton's desk. He

watched, fascinated, as the woman with gauzy, translucent butterfly wings on the magazine cover fluttered her wings.

". . . state facility . . ." Dr. Swanson said.

". . . indefinite period . . ." Dr. Milton said.

The Reverend Mr. Hobson ushered his wife to the door.

"So be it," he said disgustedly, slamming the door behind them.

Matthew watched as the woman on the magazine cover rippled her wings and flew away in a burst of brilliant color.

Matthew withdrew deeper and deeper into himself. His delusions imprisoned him, his senses lied to him. He kept his perceptions a secret, not knowing whether they would be believed, not knowing whether he believed them himself.

Odors were exaggerated or distorted. Fried chicken, brought on Sundays by another inmate's family, made him mad with hunger one week, nauseated the next.

His mind invented odors and defined them to him in outrageous terms. For an entire week he could smell the North Star, even during the day.

By state law, patients were required to exercise daily.

Usually this meant walking the perimeter of the courtyard, under the eaves of the dormitories. But on clear days the patients were taken for walks along the country roads surrounding the asylum, chained two by two at the waist. Matthew's senses were overloaded; after a walk he would be so agitated that he lay awake all night, colors and shapes dancing in front of his eyes in kaleidoscope.

After exercise came baths. Steam rose in billows from the tiled sarcophagi filled with Epsom salts and water. Violent patients might be tied into the tubs, their heads held above the water with stocks laid across the tub walls. After a patient had soaked for a quarter of an hour, he was removed, wrapped in sheets, and sent scurrying down the cold tile floors to the ward. Another patient—and another, and another—was put into the increasingly grimy water and left to his own resources while attendants saw to their duties elsewhere.

Matthew's first coherent thoughts were of suicide. He even looked around the ward for ways to do it. He stole medication from two other patients and hid the pills beneath his pillow, but the ward orderly found them when he came with fresh sheets.

If truth be told, Matthew didn't think he could have

taken the pills anyway. He was afraid for his mortal soul. He was afraid of his father. He was afraid of God. He was afraid that they were one and the same. He was afraid to find out.

It came to him that he was, after all, being punished. He was compelled to find something lost, something he would know when he laid his hands on it, something for which he had been responsible.

He started to walk the halls, rummaging through his own belongings and those of other inmates, looking, looking.

In early March his fingers were badly cut as he reached inside another inmate's suitcase. The other man slammed the case shut, and Matthew's fingers were bruised purple-green at the knuckles as they were crushed between the two halves. The other inmate laughed as Matthew howled with pain.

The guards came running. They immediately put both patients into muff restraints.

The muff was a tube of canvas fabric with straps on each end, and an additional flap of canvas inside that divided the interior of the muff into two chambers. Matthew's hands were passed through the muff and locked in on either side of the divider, which effectively separated his arms and held them overlapped across his chest.

As Matthew's throbbing hands crossed his body, his mind explained the experience to him. Matthew's favorite book as a child had been his mother's Bible; the beautiful color plates illustrated the stories he had heard from his father and brought them alive. He had particularly loved and remembered a portrait of the imprisoned Christ standing before Pilate, his hands bound before him and his head bowed in dignified submission.

The young Matthew had found the illustration wrenching. The older Matthew took it to heart. Whenever the muff was applied, he became that Christ, his head silently bowed for the souls of his persecutors as he was led back to his bed.

"Return to sender."

Zack scowled at the handwritten return notice on the letter he had mailed three weeks before to Matthew. He turned the letter over in his hands, examining the envelope for more clues. Why was his letter to Matthew being returned, unopened?

Matthew's routine, designed to quiet his turbulent mind, instead fed his madness. The doctors were too busy, the guards too indifferent to spend time with him, so he occupied himself conversing with patients whose toehold on reality was even more tenuous than his.

The daily newspapers they pored over in the ward only fueled Matthew's suspicions that great conspiracies were lurking outside the hospital walls. Why else would he have been left here? The suspicion was confirmed by the paranoids around him.

Writing and drawing materials—soft charcoals and grainy paper—were also available in the ward. But to whom would he write? His father had abandoned him. The school life he had shared with Cappy was now miles and years behind him. Zack would be shamed to know what he had done. There was no one else.

Meals were a special torment.

Breakfast was a watery oat gruel without milk or sugar. At dinner the bread was brick. It was served with thin greasy soup, heavily laced with pepper and salt to give an illusion of flavor.

The meat served with the four o'clock supper was purchased from local butchers who wanted to unload cuts too poor to sell to the area's schools and restaurants but too good to go to the rendering plant—although not by much.

Each meal became a ritual: A guard carried in the

food tray and held a spoon full of gray food under Matthew's nose. Matthew began to turn his head away.

The guard, not keen on hand-feeding the boy in the first place, left, taking the tray with him to the guards' dayroom.

After a week of starvation Matthew was severely dehydrated and disoriented. Two of the guards assigned to the ward, finally fearing the wrath of the superintendent and the possible loss of their easy jobs, realized that it was in their own best interests to fatten the boy up.

The older guard, a former dockworker named Hammner, decided to act. He asked his wife to pack up a bowl of her mulligan stew, a pungent broth thick with tomatoes, potatoes, celery, onion slices, and chunks of beef.

"Want it, boy?" Hammner asked, waving the bowl under Matthew's nose.

Matthew stared straight ahead. He was starving, but the food smelled strange and tainted to his damaged perceptions.

"Here. Take it," Hammner insisted.

Matthew looked at the bowl but said nothing. He wanted to ask about the odd odor, but he no longer had the use of words.

Matthew slouched down on his bed. No words

came, even in his thoughts. He had shut out all language, abandoned it.

As a child Matthew had been shy, self-conscious. He envied other little boys their glib, smart-aleck ways. Matthew strove for invisibility.

In his father's church he had dreaded the time when his father would call for testimony from the congregation. He trembled, fearing that his father might call on him to confess some childish prank—though Matthew had been too timid to ever partake in such innocent fun. The thought of doing wrong was as sinful as the act itself, and Matthew knew it. Confession brought punishment—and even worse, ridicule.

If he spoke now, Matthew might, and probably would, say something that would shame him even further or incriminate him even deeper in the crimes of which he was accused. Words would give his adversaries ammunition with which to persecute him. Words would betray him.

Hammner held the spoon against Matthew's lips, but the boy turned his head away silently.

"He's been struck dumb," the other guard said, taking the bowl and eating the stew himself. Matthew watched him, miserable hunger in his eyes.

"He'll learn to talk when he gets hungry enough," Hammner growled as he closed the door.

Matthew ate now only when he was force-fed, and a nurse was assigned to feed him twice daily. Matthew would open his mouth for the approaching spoon of gritty morning oatmeal or salty evening stew but would not swallow. The nurse forced him to swallow by stroking his throat.

This ritual was performed without conversation or interchange between nurse and patient. The nurse had six inmates to feed at each meal, and Matthew would be fed as expediently as possible. Her job was filling his stomach; his mind was not her problem.

And as if the callousness of the guards was not enough, Matthew's anguished mind added its own torments.

Folded at the foot of his bed was a woolen comforter with a long soft fringe, a gift from his mother surreptitiously sent through Dr. Swanson. The comforter became a small soft dog snuggled in his lap, and he would stroke it for hours, humming softly to himself.

One afternoon Matthew awoke from a light sleep and saw that the "dog" had awakened before him and lay growling at the foot of his bed. He reached his hand toward it, and the dog snarled viciously. A drop of blood which Matthew knew was his own appeared at the corner of the dog's mouth.

Matthew recoiled in horror. The dog stood, and

Matthew could clearly see that the spot where the dog had laid on the coverlet was soaked with Matthew's blood. He watched, terrified, as the dog advanced on him. It sprang for his throat.

Matthew put his arms out and caught the dog in midair. He pushed the dog down on the bed and held it there as it snarled and snapped at him. Finally the dog lay still.

Matthew looked down at his hands. The skin of his hands and arms was entirely gloved with the dog's ticks, each swollen with a gorge of blood.

Matthew screamed. The attendant came in and untangled the comforter from his arms.

Matthew did not stop screaming.

The man left the room, carrying the comforter with him.

"Seclusion," the guard said to the attendant in the hall.

```
YOUR MAIL RETURNED STOP IS ALL
WELL STOP WIRE IF YOU NEED ME STOP
ZACK
```

Cappy signed for the telegram and took it at once to Dr. Swanson.

"See," Cappy said, holding out the telegram. "I told you his brother would come looking for him."

A search of Matthew's belongings had turned up no

trace of Zack's postcard, and Cappy hadn't been able to remember the name of the town where Zack had the ranch. And, of course, Matthew's parents had refused to give the doctor any information.

Dr. Swanson looked at the dateline on the telegram: Carter, Colorado.

"I'll wire him right away," the doctor said.

It was cold. Matthew's teeth chattered, and his eyes were rolled partway back into his head. He fought to regain consciousness.

The padded cell was six feet square, with walls twenty feet tall padded as high as Matthew could have reached with his fingertips—had his hands been free. Inside, Matthew sat on the floor, wearing only underwear and a straitjacket.

The guard. Something about the guard. Yes, the guard had done something that . . .

He had been choked, that was it. The guard had come in and flipped Matthew over in the bed, then worked an arm under Matthew's neck and pressed up against his carotid. Matthew's horror of the ticks had vanished behind the very real fear of dying at the guard's hands. He had started to scream, but the air was cut off.

Don't fight, he had thought. It will only make things worse. He had been fully lucid as he blacked out.

There were no windows, no way to tell how much time had passed. But the burning of his muscles inside the straitjacket gave him a rough idea.

After several hours the peephole in the door opened and a face appeared. A few muffled sounds and conversation outside, and Dr. Harrison was ordering that the door be opened.

". . . no restraint without orders from the doctor in charge," he said to whoever was standing outside the door. "Am I understood?"

There was a mumbled reply outside, then the shuffling of feet away down the corridor. Dr. Harrison and an attendant Matthew had never seen before helped Matthew to his feet, but he was unable to stand alone.

"Back in his bed," the doctor said over his shoulder as he left without looking at Matthew.

Matthew lay on the bed, sheets encasing him tightly from the waist down. From the waist up he wore a straitjacket. His arms were numb; his hands tingled.

The ward was filled with sleep sounds: the loud snoring and troubled mumbled dreams of the other patients. Outside in the corridor a man screamed once, then all was quiet.

Matthew's eyes were open, glistening, uncomprehending. He blinked, unfocused, at the ceiling as the clock ticked inside its wire cage above the door.

CHAPTER

Zack took the steps of the college admissions office two at a time.

"Hobson," he said to the clerk at the desk. "Matthew Hobson."

The woman consulted a file, then opened a ledger on the desk. "That's odd," she said. "He's not on our student rolls for this term, but he's never officially withdrawn."

"What does that mean?"

"It could mean any number of things." She smiled. "Most likely it's a clerical error. Maybe he forgot to turn in his forms when he dropped out."

"He hasn't dropped out," Zack said, remembering Matthew's panic when Zack had even suggested it. "Your Dr. Swanson wired me that he was ill."

"Well, there's no record of him in the current class

rolls." She glanced at a door at the far end of the office. "Wait here a minute," she said kindly.

She disappeared through the door marked Dean of Admissions. A few minutes later she was back; she seemed more subdued, cautious.

"I'm sorry," she said, and it sounded genuine. "There isn't anything more I can tell you. If you'd like to make an appointment with the dean for tomorrow, perhaps . . ."

"Never mind," Zack snapped.

Cappy sat bolt upright in bed, his nap interrupted, trying to understand the pounding that filled the room. Zack beat on the door again.

Cappy sprang from the bed and let him in.

"What happened?" Zack demanded. "Where's my brother?"

"You're Zack, right?" Cappy stammered, still rousing from his deep sleep.

Zack nodded.

Cappy shivered. He grabbed his robe from the foot of the bed and put it on. "We've been trying to find you," he told Zack.

"My letters came back," Zack replied. "And then when I got the telegram from your doctor, here . . . Where is Matthew? What's going on?"

"He was kicked out," Cappy said flatly.

"God," Zack said.

"Yeah," Cappy agreed.

"The admissions office won't tell me anything," Zack said, his frustration edging his voice, "and the doctor is off somewhere."

"Zack, Matthew is in the asylum."

"What?" Zack exploded.

"When he got expelled, he sort of collapsed," Cappy said quickly. "It was awful, Zack. He sort of went numb. He wouldn't talk or eat or anything. They moved him out of here just like a big rag-doll."

"Jesus."

"Yeah. The doc says it's a good place, out at the edge of town . . ."

Zack was starting to realize what was being told to him. "There's nothing wrong with my brother's mind," he said under his breath.

"Zack," Cappy said gently, "getting all wrought up won't help. What's done is done. Besides, they say he's some better since they took him out there."

"You haven't seen him?"

"They won't let me in," Cappy replied.

"Why didn't the doctor just keep him here at school?" Zack demanded.

"He's in a bad way, Zack. You've got to understand.

The doctor says sometimes he's like a little baby, but scared all the time. They're just not set up to deal with it here. They had to hold him in the jail over in town until the doc could get him in at the asylum."

Zack's eyes were flint. "Where is this doctor?"

Cappy reached for his pocket watch on the desk and squinted at it. "Maybe he's back at the infirmary by now. I'll go over with you."

Dr. Swanson was just taking off his coat when Zack stalked into the infirmary, Cappy being dragged behind like a dinghy being towed by a ship.

"This is Matthew's brother," Cappy gasped breathlessly to the doctor.

Zack, calmer after the fast walk across campus, extended his hand. "Zack Hobson," he said. "Much obliged for your wire."

"Glad we found you," the doctor replied, shaking Zack's hand. "Your brother really needs family right now."

Dr. Swanson gave Zack a brief description of Matthew's condition and told him about the visit by the Reverend Mr. Hobson and his wife.

Zack's face was flat with controlled anger. "So my father's abandoned him."

"That's about it," Dr. Swanson agreed.

"Can I see him? Will he know me?"

"I doubt it, and I'm not sure they'll let you in there, even with me," the doctor said. "Matthew isn't able to speak for himself. Your father is still his legal guardian, you know. If he wants you kept out . . ."

"We'll get in," Zack said firmly.

Matthew watched the rain spatter on the big bay window all afternoon. As the day wore on, he began to see that the rivulets of water formed patterns on the outside of the glass. The heat from the radiator below the window steamed the inner pane; droplets of condensation formed on the inside, intersecting, joining, and splitting again as they fell.

Matthew watched, fascinated. By evening he knew that the rivulets were forming words, words he could not read but that he knew specified the charges against him. He rose from the bed and wiped the steam from the pane with his nightshirt sleeve as one would clear a school slate. The steam and droplets reappeared, but Matthew still could not decipher their meaning as he fretted himself to restless sleep.

"I'm sorry, Mr. Hobson," Dr. Harrison said reasonably, "but Matthew is unable to have visitors at this time."

"But I'm his brother," Zack insisted. "I want to see how he's doing." Zack looked at Dr. Swanson but got only an I-told-you-so shrug.

Dr. Harrison smiled pleasantly. "We just can't allow him to be upset at this point in his treatment. His condition is very delicate. And, of course, we would need permission from his guardian."

"His guardian doesn't care if he lives or dies," Zack said matter-of-factly.

"Your father has the final decision in this case."

Zack threw up his hands in frustration. "Well, can I at least write him a letter? Will he get it?"

"That is at the discretion of your father, and your brother's doctors," Dr. Harrison said.

"So it always comes back to him," Zack said bitterly.

"I'm afraid so." Dr. Harrison smiled. "Now, is there anything else I can do for you gentlemen?"

The train ride to Brookbend had done little to improve Zack's mood, but he had worked off most of his anger by the time he got there. What was left was pure determination. The law offices of Hamilton P. Kramer were only a short walk from the trolley stop.

If anyone could get through to his father, Zack thought, it would be Ham Kramer.

The church, of course, retained an expensive law

firm for its official work. But over the years his father had occasionally found it convenient to seek advice from someone on the outside, and Kramer had given that advice for two decades, trusted as an advisor if not exactly welcomed as a family friend.

The arrangement was strictly business; the elder Hobson had sought out an attorney who was expressly not a member of the congregation to which he ministered, someone whose advice would not be colored by any other loyalties.

Ham Kramer filled the bill nicely. He talked straight to his clients, even if it wasn't the advice they wanted to hear. And he was a member of Beth Israel Conservative Congregation over on Center Street, a satisfyingly long distance both culturally and theologically from the Reverend Mr. Hobson's pulpit. They had had many fallings-out over the years, but Zack's father respected Ham Kramer's advice over that of most others.

The lawyer listened without comment to Zack's story. He raised one furry eyebrow when Zack related the preacher's visit to the asylum, and clucked in sympathy as Zack described his brother's plight.

When Zack finished, Kramer sat studying Zack's face.

"And so, what do you want to do now?" he asked.

"That's what I was hoping you could tell me," Zack replied.

The lawyer pulled down a book. "I'm not sure we can do anything for your brother," he began. Zack started to rise from his chair; Kramer put a comforting hand on his shoulder.

"But," he continued as he pushed Zack back down, "there are a few things we can try." Zack relaxed a bit as Kramer pointed to a passage in the book.

"Conservatorship," Zack read.

"That means you become the caretaker of Matthew's estate, responsible for him."

"I thought my father was his guardian."

"That's where it gets sticky," the lawyer explained. "We have to convince him to cede custody to you, for Matthew's own good."

"He doesn't care about Matthew's good. What if he refuses?"

Kramer sighed. "Then we would have to petition the court to make you conservator. We would have to show that your father does not have Matthew's best interests at heart."

"He'd fight it, to protect his own reputation."

"Then you'd better have proof. Solid proof."

Zack shook his head. "I don't want to go toe-to-toe with him in court. It could get real bad."

Kramer agreed. "It would be best if you could talk to him, let him know what you want to do. He probably won't agree, but it will look better in court if you try."

"Go over there?"

Kramer nodded. "See him, face-to-face."

"Can't you talk to him first?" Zack asked.

"Zack, this is between you and your father. If he says no, then I'll start the petition. I can't get into a conflict of interest here; I don't want to talk to him unless I'm officially representing you. I'll call him if we file."

"You don't know what you're asking."

"I think I do."

Zack felt goose bumps on his arms as the trolley rounded the corner and he saw the parsonage. He sat on a bench across the street, looking at the house where he had grown up.

It looked the same.

Six years, Zack thought, since he had stormed out of this house. The trees were taller, and there was a new fence behind the back porch. But the parsonage still looked as it did in his memory, all white clapboard and sturdy brick chimneys.

His father's house.

There was a flicker of movement at the window. They had seen him.

Zack had planned to march up onto the porch, bang on the door, and demand that his father release Matthew to him. Now action failed him.

It was a sensation strange to Zack, who had gotten used to getting what he wanted. But he had hesitated this time and lost the advantage of surprise.

Hat in hand, he walked up to the door and rang the bell. There was a shuffle inside, but no one answered.

Zack knocked on the door. The house was quiet, but Zack sensed that there was someone by the door. He stood his ground.

Inside the house, Mrs. Hobson had her hand on the doorknob. Her husband stood beside her, the pressure of his hand over hers on the knob tightening. She winced but kept her hand in place.

With his other hand the Reverend Mr. Hobson removed her grasp from the doorknob.

"No," he said firmly.

Elizabeth Hobson pleaded with her eyes, knowing that words would lose her the battle.

The Reverend Mr. Hobson looked away and led her back toward the kitchen.

"I'll not have him in my house," he said.

Mrs. Hobson shook her head. "You yourself tell the story about the prodigal returning . . ."

"Not the prodigal. The infidel—on the Devil's own business. You're not to open that door."

He held his wife's hand in his powerful grip. She was overwhelmed by his presence, the power of him. She nodded assent.

With grim satisfaction he returned her nod as he went into his study and closed the door.

Tears formed in Elizabeth Hobson's eyes as, peeking through the lace curtain, she saw her oldest child stalk off in anger.

Zack rang up Ham Kramer from the lobby of his hotel.

"He won't see me," Zack told the lawyer across the crackling line.

"What did you expect?" Kramer asked. "Your father is a stubborn man. But we had to try."

"File the petition," Zack said.

"Are you sure?" Kramer asked, his voice full of caution.

"File it."

From the park bench around the corner, Zack had a clear view of the parsonage.

He checked his pocket watch: ten-thirty.

Soon, soon.

He rubbed the morning chill from his hands, then peeled the brown paper from one of the muffins he'd brought from the hotel dining room. He ate without taking his eyes from the parsonage door.

Just as he finished the muffin, the door opened, and the Reverend Mr. Hobson stepped on to the porch. Zack was shocked at how gray his father's hair had become. But the older man was still straight-shouldered and rigid in his bearing.

More than half a decade, Zack thought, since he had turned his back on this house and strode confidently up this street and out of town, out of this life.

Zack and his father had clashed constantly, almost from the time Zack learned to talk. He shared his father's ardor for causes and his stubborn refusal to yield to any other point of view.

As the boys grew up, Zack became Matthew's champion against their father—as much for the potential for confrontation as for Matthew's sake, Zack now suspected.

War was inevitable, and the final battle came two weeks after Zack graduated from high school. Although neither would have admitted it, not father nor son could now remember the topic of the argument. But at the time the confrontation had been all-important, ending with Zack overturning the breakfast table into his father's lap and stomping from the house.

Two hours later Zack had found himself in front of the train station. At noon he was on a train steaming west across the open prairie; he had neither topcoat nor luggage, nor even a hat.

Six years, Zack thought. He watched as the Reverend Mr. Hobson took his Bible from his wife and left the porch. The set of the jaw was the same, the profile, the square of the shoulders.

Zack held his breath, hoping that his father wouldn't walk in his direction. He relaxed when the preacher veered off to the left at the foot of the walk and strolled up toward the center of town. Zack watched him go until he disappeared beyond the crest of the farthest hill, ten blocks away.

His mother opened the door before he stepped up onto the porch. She flung her arms around him and buried her head in his shoulder. She did not cry. She did not laugh.

He smoothed her hair and tried to comfort her as she clung to him. Finally she released him and, leading him by the hand, brought him into her house.

"I'm going to take him out to the ranch," Zack said, munching another cookie as they sat in the warm kitchen.

"Your father will never stand for it," his mother said sadly, shaking her head.

"My father won't have any say in the matter," Zack said grimly.

Elizabeth Hobson looked at her oldest child. So like his father, she thought: the confident eyes, the squared stance, the sure knowledge that he was right. How could they both be right? she wondered. And how could she choose between them?

"Matthew is going with me," Zack was saying, "and that's the end of it. That ranch is half his. It's in his name. Father has no right to keep him locked up."

"Your father feels that Matthew's troubles are of his own choosing," Elizabeth said. "He feels that Matthew can pull himself out of this if he wants to."

"That's ridiculous!" Zack exploded. "Cappy says he's like a kicked puppy! Have you seen him?"

Elizabeth nodded miserably.

"It's all his doing," Zack said, tossing his head toward his father's study.

Elizabeth put her arms around her son's shoulders. No little boy now that she could pull up onto her lap and comfort. The days were gone when she could kiss his forehead and push his troubles aside.

"It's big out there, open," Zack said, his eyes seeing a thousand miles. He held up her hand and touched the stone in his grandmother's sapphire ring on her finger. "The sky is like this."

Elizabeth looked into the depths of the stone and understood.

"Matthew'll be safe where I'm taking him," Zack said. It was a statement without room for question. "Even if he"—Zack nodded toward the empty study— "fights me."

She kissed his forehead.

"Kiss Matthew for me," she said.

Elizabeth caught herself daydreaming as the choir sang that evening. In her mind she saw green wheat fields on an open prairie, and a sky the color of her mother's ring. Her praise was real and heartfelt as she joined the responses to the litany.

Matthew would be safe.

Amen.

CHAPTER

As Zack sat in the lawyer's office, Matthew was being transferred to hell.

Matthew had occasional moments of clarity now when the real world appeared in bright-edged relief. It was during such a moment that the ward attendants came to make their bed check and found Edgar Potter in the corridor, crying.

Potter, seventy-three, had lived within the asylum since it had been built fifteen years before. His original diagnosis had been alcoholism; in the first three years of his voluntary commitment, he had at various times drunk lamp alcohol, laudanum syrup, and finally wood alcohol from the paint locker.

This last binge had ulcerated his stomach and left him blind in one eye and with only dim sight in the other. The damage to his brain had also immobilized his left side, so that he dragged his leg along behind him.

The guards found Potter, now called The Crab, to be an easy target. They vented their frustrations on him over the least infraction. As senility added itself to the other insults his body had suffered, Potter lost control even over his bodily functions. The beatings were now administered daily.

Matthew opened his eyes that day to The Crab's helpless screams. The guards had found the old man crouched naked against the corridor wall, finger painting with his own excrement. Their attack was sudden and brutal.

Matthew's hands were bound in a muff, but his legs were free. He kicked off the blankets and stood shakily. His feet made no sound as he padded across the cold tiles.

The guards were preoccupied with The Crab, their backs to the ward door. Matthew moved across the corridor and, without warning or hesitation, kicked the larger guard squarely between the legs from behind.

The guard dropped like a rock. "Get him," he gasped to his partner.

The old man forgotten, the second guard turned on Matthew. Matthew saw a giant fist coming at his left temple—then blackness.

The violent ward was beyond nightmare. Matthew had been stripped to his underwear and put, unconscious, into a big dimly lit room with high airless windows. Along the walls were wooden benches, bolted to the floor so they could not be thrown. There were no pads on the wall, no cots, not even pillows or blankets.

The room was icy cold, as low temperature was believed to be soothing to violent patients. In reality the chill set already sensitive nerve endings resonating with pain.

Some of the patients on the ward were truly violent; their brutal, uncontrollable outbursts of anger were vented against the other patients on the ward, usually with indifference from the guards.

Also on the ward were patients who were in "elation," a heightened sensitivity marked by constant movement and talking.

These men chattered endlessly, sharing their great revelations. They slept only a few hours after sundown; for the rest of the night they would pace and talk. When boredom overtook them, they howled at the moon until another patient beat them into submission.

They too were sometimes violent, but there was no malice in their brutality. They could—and did—exude joy even as they broke another patient's arm.

Patients were introduced to the violent ward by an attendant named Fists, a former circus roustabout who had been hired to keep the peace. Fists made it a general practice to assault patients on their first day on the ward, to teach them who was in charge.

Bruises could be easily explained in the violent ward, and Fists was a master at finding just the right spot to inflict pain without breaking bones. This he usually did with a broom handle, or sometimes with his keys.

It worked. Patients cringed and quickly moved away as Fists entered the ward and purposefully advanced on Matthew.

Matthew saw the broom handle as it hit his arm just above the elbow. Fists grinned as he left the ward.

That night Matthew dreamed he was flying over the rooftops. He awoke in a straitjacket.

Matthew turned his head and could see The Crab in the next bed. The old man had been beaten senseless; spots of blood marred the cot. His eyes were blackened and swollen shut. Matthew could see no muff or straitjacket.

Dr. Harrison came in with a young doctor Matthew had never seen before. They gave The Crab a cursory examination.

". . . restrained with hyoscine," Matthew heard one of them say. So that was it. Matthew had heard talk in the dayroom about hyoscine. The patients thought it came from the Amazon, some kind of poison used by the natives. It paralyzed the body completely for a short time. Poor old man.

Matthew's arms were numb within the straitjacket when he awoke. He tried to move them, to get the blood circulating, but the jacket arms were tied too tight. He was completely immobilized.

The numbness was bad, but what followed was infinitely worse. Sensation returned to his shoulders, then to his upper arms, his elbows, forearms, and hands. But this was not normal feeling; it was a burning, tearing cramp that was rending muscle from bone within the jacket. Matthew screamed in agony. No one came.

Edgar "The Crab" Potter did not move for the rest of the day. Matthew's screams diminished as the scraps of reason he had regained left him again. He whimpered softly as the evening light faded from the room.

The process server delivered the custody petition to the parsonage at one-twenty on a bright Tuesday afternoon. At one-thirty the phone rang at the law offices.

"How dare you, sir!" the preacher roared through the static.

Ham Kramer winced.

"Andrew!" he said in his courtroom voice. "How are you today?"

"You know very well how I am. What is the meaning of this?"

The lawyer steeled himself. "It's written clear enough, Andrew. Zack is asking to be conservator for Matthew."

"Zack has no say in this matter."

"He thinks differently, Andrew. He is the boy's brother, after all."

The preacher harrumphed. "Brother, indeed. He's doing this to embarrass me, is all. That boy never cared two figs about anyone in his life."

"He's genuinely concerned, Andrew, and he's worried that Matthew isn't getting proper care."

"The boy will be fine," the preacher said flatly.

"Will he, Andrew? Have you been out there lately to check on him? Because legally you are the only one who can."

"Matthew will be fine when he comes to his senses and does his duty."

"Duty?" The lawyer fought to keep the anger from his voice. "Duty to whom? That boy needs help, someone to look out for him until he's able to manage on his own."

"I will pray for him to be given guidance and strength, but it's up to him to pull himself together—and I want you to know, I resent your interference, Hamilton Kramer."

"I'm telling you as a friend, Andrew: Matthew needs understanding, not preaching," the lawyer said gently.

"He needs to let Jesus back into his heart," the preacher replied firmly, "something you are not qualified to discuss."

Kramer held his breath, waiting for the anti-Semitic slur which would end a twenty-year relationship.

But the preacher kept his silence.

"If you turn your back on Matthew now, you'll lose him," Kramer said.

The preacher said nothing. Kramer listened to the crackle of the lines for a moment, then continued. "Zack wants to take the boy and look after him. If you can't have him with you and your wife, then maybe . . ."

"He can go with his brother, or go to the Devil for all I care. He's turned his back on God's will. 'If thine eye offend thee, pluck it out.' "

"Or cut off your nose to spite your face," the lawyer retorted, disgusted. "Sign the papers and you'll be rid of them both then."

"Send your messenger at four o'clock," the preacher said as he hung up.

When the doctor came in for rounds the next morning, he found the color in Matthew's gums and nose membranes nearly white. He ordered the straitjacket removed.

The guards were called. Matthew was unable to move his arms and legs; the muscles would not respond. After twenty hours in the jacket he had no muscle control. His fingernails were purple against his pale skin.

"You'll be all right," a guard said with a laugh. "Just need some time to get the old feeling back."

Matthew lay motionless on the bed. His muscles had already begun to cramp from the unaccustomed movement after so many hours.

There was a commotion at the bed beside his. Edgar, The Crab, was dead.

CHAPTER

Zack presented the custody papers an hour later at the asylum. Dr. Milton read them carefully, then curtly asked Zack to have a seat in his office. The doctor disappeared down the hallway.

Forty minutes later the doctor returned and brusquely reintroduced Dr. Harrison. Together they reread the papers, occasionally looking up at Zack as if he had come to loot their safe.

"I assure you, they are in order," Zack said impatiently as the doctors shuffled the last of the onionskin sheets into a pile. "Now when can I see my brother?"

"We have wired your father for confirmation," Dr. Milton began. "We'll have his answer shortly." He stood to show Zack back to the waiting room.

"My father! You can wait until hell freezes over, and he'll never answer!"

The doctor took a step backward. Zack forced himself into the chair.

"Gentlemen," he said, trying to sound reasonable, "you have both dealt with my father. Do you really believe that he would reply to your telegram?"

The doctors exchanged looks.

"We can't just release the boy without the proper permissions," Dr. Milton began. "We would be liable . . ."

"But you have the papers right there in your hand," Zack said.

Both doctors shrugged.

"At least let me see my brother," Zack said. "You can at least let me do that."

Dr. Milton hesitated for a moment. Dr. Harrison nodded, and Dr. Milton pressed a buzzer on his desk. An electric bell sounded in the corridor, and in a few seconds an attendant came into the room.

"Where is Matthew Hobson right now?" Dr. Milton asked.

"In the baths, I think," the attendant answered.

"Bring him to my examining room," the doctor ordered.

The attendant left, closing the door behind him.

"It will be a few minutes," Dr. Milton said.

"I'll wait," Zack said.

Matthew was brought into a small, clean room next to Dr. Milton's office. Dr. Milton gave him a hurried examination while an orderly stood by, and then returned to his office, leaving Matthew alone with his guard.

Matthew listened to the quiet for a few moments. Suddenly through the partly open door came muffled angry shouting.

"You have the papers there! I'm taking him, and that's all there is to it."

"This is very irregular, very irregular," came Dr. Harrison's measured voice.

Matthew's guard cocked his head toward the door, gathering in the conversation for future gossip. Matthew did not dare show any interest.

In Matthew's perception the conversation was only disembodied voices. There were the voices of the doctors, but there was another too, a voice half-heard, half-remembered.

". . . his brother."

There was quiet discussion for a moment. Then the eavesdropping guard heard Dr. Milton speak.

"His father told us that the brother was dead."

"Do I look dead to you?" Zack exploded.

Another muffled conference.

"Look," said Zack, exasperated. "I don't care what

he told you. I have it there, all legal. I'm Matthew's guardian now, and he's going with me."

He paused. "Besides," he said coldly, "you already said they refused to pay for his keep."

"He's scheduled to go to the state hospital tomorrow afternoon," Dr. Milton said noncommittally.

"I've got train tickets for Colorado tonight."

"But he's in no condition to travel that far," Dr. Harrison objected.

"That's right," Dr. Milton joined in. "We can't be responsible."

"Then discharge him to me," Zack insisted.

There was more murmuring. The doctors were talking it over.

To Matthew there was no sense to it. The only word he understood in his drugged haze was "Colorado," but it produced no emotion, no reaction.

The three men came into the examining room. Zack was shocked. His brother's hair hung in wet, greasy strands over glazed, drugged eyes. The boy's arms showed angry chafe burns. He lay motionless on the table.

Matthew did not look up when Zack embraced him.

"We might release him to you as improved but not

recovered. Would you sign to that effect?" asked Dr. Harrison.

Dr. Milton gestured toward Matthew. "As you can see, he won't know where he is or what he's about. He is a vegetable."

Zack's voice was grim as he turned on the doctors. "All sorts of things grow where I'm taking him."

Matthew's view as he was carried to the waiting ambulance was severely limited by the cot to which he was strapped and by the rough woolen blankets in which he had been wrapped for warmth and restraint.

It didn't matter. He paid little attention to the four large attendants who carried him through the wards for the last time. He heard only the assault of their shoes slapping along the concrete floors. The ceiling passed above his head, with an occasional hanging lamp fixture in distorted perspective swaying into and out of his line of sight.

The floorboards on the veranda made a hollow sound underfoot, and then his bearers were crunching across a gravel drive.

There was suddenly color—an amber sunset sky, and green trees. It was a shock to Matthew, after all his months inside the gray asylum. He could smell the horses as his litter bearers carried him up to the cavernous ambulance. Then the light changed again, and he was sliding into the dark recess, disembodied voices swirling in from outside.

"Thank you," he heard Zack say. "I know you did the best you could."

What was he talking about? Matthew wondered. Who was he talking to?

Two other voices, sounding embarrassed, mumbled unintelligible words.

Zack was beside him then, sitting next to the cot. The doors closed. The only light came from a small window behind the driver. Zack steadied the cot. Matthew closed his eyes as the ambulance began to rock across the uneven pavement.

Zack looked down at his brother, trundled immobile in the cot. At Matthew's feet was his steamer trunk.

What have I gotten myself into? Zack wondered.

He loosened the blankets and tried to make Matthew more comfortable, but Matthew did not seem to care.

They passed a church, and Zack could hear organ music. The station was just ahead.

A closed door in Matthew's mind was unsealed for a moment as the organ music reached it. He opened his eyes.

The inside of the ambulance was dark. The blankets cocooned him, kept him safe; his mind felt them only as the enfolding sound of the chapel organ. The music floated him along until it was replaced by the insistent chugging of train wheels.

The train trip west was, fortunately, uneventful. Most of the time Matthew slept.

Each day Zack got him up in the morning and dressed him. Zack, thinking it was not good for the boy to linger in bed, would put his arm around his brother's waist and walk him to the dining car for breakfast. Matthew chewed the food Zack placed in his mouth but would not feed himself. Zack ignored the stares of the other passengers.

After breakfast Zack would help Matthew to a seat in the coach car. Matthew would not respond to Zack's comments on the passing countryside but stared out the window until it was again time for bed.

Zack watched wearily out the window as the train approached Carter, Colorado. To the west the town sat in a half circle of mountains, the foot of the Rockies. To the east the prairie smoothed out, gouged here and there by a rocky arroyo.

Far off to the south, Zack could see billows of oily black smoke rising from a deep canyon. An outsider might think there was a brush fire, but Zack knew different. In Chili Canyon was a coal mine and a furnace, burning coal into coke for the steel mills at Pueblo. In that canyon was backbreaking work and little pay, sweltering heat, and sometimes violent death. Zack knew because it was in that canyon he'd earned his stake for the ranch.

Zack's first shift on the coke ovens had been the longest day of his life. The simmering blast seared the fine hairs from his face and made his eyes ache. His muscles burned from the weight of the scraper and the coke fork. When he collapsed into his rented room in one of the tiny adobes, his $1.80 wages duly credited on the company books, he dreamed of Brookbend, and of cool river water.

And then one blistering July day Zack found a notice posted at the general merchandise store in Trinidad, advertising that Mr. Abner Wilson would buy wilded cattle for a dollar a head.

Every season, cattle ranches lost a few head to storms, a few more to predators, and a few that just wandered off, never to be seen again. Those cattle, turned wild, found forage in the high mesa scrub and learned to avoid man. They were wily, free and determined to stay that way.

Rounding up wilded cattle involved riding near-vertical hillsides, then herding—or chasing—the cattle back down. Sometimes a recalcitrant steer would turn and charge; then horse and rider needed to look sharp to come out ungored. A rider might spend an entire day chasing one animal, only to find that the quarry had disappeared through the blind end of a canyon without a trace.

Zack took his money from the mine and talked the livery into staking him to a twenty-five-dollar horse. His first day out, Zack got three steers and two saddle sores. He had burrs all through his clothes and hair. He hurt in places he'd forgotten he owned. He was exhausted—but he was three dollars richer.

Zack worked the ovens during the night and searched the high country each morning. He slept four hours at dawn, four at sunset. Within a month he had paid off his horse, and his bank account began to grow.

He recognized the property the first time he saw it, as if he had lived there all his life. The man at the bank had mentioned that a family from the East, tired of trying to learn to farm the unforgiving prairie, had decided to give up and go home. The bank was looking for someone to buy their property and to pay off the loan they had taken out for seed. The banker offered it to Zack.

The first two years were hard. Zack kept his job at the coke ovens, but now his days were ranch work: fences and ditches and keeping the land cleared. The third year, he had two fields in alfalfa and had sold enough to quit the mines for good.

Now, five years later, it was Zack who bought wilded cattle from itinerant cowboys. He had built up the ranch himself, for himself and Matthew. At last, as he watched from the train window and saw the smoke rise over Chili Canyon, he was bringing Matthew home.

George Harper, Zack's foreman, met Zack and Matthew at the station in Carter. Together Zack and George half-supported, half-carried Matthew down the platform to Zack's yellow truck. They laid him in the truck bed for the ten-mile drive out to the ranch.

"Remember the truck, Matthew? Someday you'll be driving it all over the county," Zack said.

George looked down at Matthew, who had quickly fallen asleep. "What's wrong with the boy?" he asked.

"Too much good Christian charity." Zack's face was grim as he climbed up onto the truck seat beside George. "Let's go," he said, pointing off into the prairie.

George drove due west, toward the place where the Rocky Mountains rose straight up from the grassy plateau floor. The dirt road ran along a creek; on either side grazed fat cattle. A brick-red mesa dominated the landscape in front of them.

A few miles later the road wound along beside the base of the mesa. Ahead, set on high ground in the shelter of a hill, was the ranch house. The main room was the original adobe house, with walls, three feet thick. Last year Zack had clad it with clapboards and added on bedrooms and a real kitchen. The house now had a timbered roof and glass windowpanes. The Navajo rugs Zack had acquired on a cattle-buying trip to Arizona were hung as blackout curtains for the sleeping rooms.

At the front of the house, Zack had built a plank porch and furnished it with two rocking chairs, even though no one ever came to call.

After five years' work the ranch was self-sufficient. On one side of the main house was a root cellar and cookshack, once the former owner's homestead; on the other side, Zack had built a bunkhouse for the crew, which numbered from three to twenty hands depending on the season. A huge barn and brick silo stood at the far end of the yard.

George looked at Matthew, who still dozed in the truck bed. "This is about the prettiest time of day to come in, I reckon. Too bad he's fast asleep."

Zack nodded at the house with satisfaction. "He'll see it."

George pulled the truck up to the porch. As Zack and the foreman got out, several huge turkeys strutted around from behind the far end of the porch.

Zack waved his arm at the birds, and they ran back behind the porch.

George laughed. "You've sure got them buffaloed."

"Yeah." Zack chuckled. "There's nothing dumber than a turkey, but they know who's in charge."

He shook Matthew's shoulder, and the boy stirred. Zack started to lift him from the truck bed.

"Here, George, give me a hand with him," he said. George took Matthew on the other side, and they helped him into the house.

George and Zack half-carried Matthew through the front door and sat him down on the sofa.

"I'll get his things," George said, heading back out the door.

Zack nudged Matthew's shoulder. "This is it, boy. We're here."

Matthew looked up at Zack without recognition. Instead he twisted his finger in the fabric of his pants leg.

"Right," said Zack resignedly.

George returned with Matthew's bags and set them down. "Take 'em on back to the extra room," Zack said, nodding down the dark hallway.

George picked up the heavy bags and shuffled down the hall as Zack, exhausted, slumped down into a big horsehair chair. On the sofa Matthew stared at his fingers.

Zack folded his arms across his chest, tipped his hat down over his eyes, and let out a deep sigh.

"And so it begins, brother," Zack said. "So it begins."

CHAPTER

Midnight.

A shadowy figure moved past the wire turkey pen, setting off startled gobbling. The silent form took no notice; he entered the barn and moved purposefully toward the chicken coops.

The coops in a quiet corner of the barn were four rows of wooden boxes, ten bins to a row, rather like the cubbyholes in a rolltop desk. The hens had nestled in for the night.

Matthew, navigating by the moonlight over his shoulder through the barn door, approached the coops. He was wearing only a nightshirt, his feet bare against the dirt floor.

His hands moved quickly through the nesting boxes, sending outraged hens squawking and scurrying for the open barn door. His eyes were frantic, out of control. He was looking for something, ignoring the raucous din of the hens.

A light was suddenly lit in the bunkhouse, but Matthew worked on, methodically going through each bin, sending the incensed hens flying. His hands were sticky now with broken eggs.

At the end of the bins Matthew stopped, confused. Muffled voices could be heard now from the bunkhouse, but Matthew never looked in that direction. He ran his hand through the last bin again, fingering the straw, trying to make the image before his eyes coincide with the one in his mind.

All at once, he was very, very sleepy. He padded off toward the house, wading, oblivious, through the sea of flustered chickens. As Matthew entered the house, Zack's crew emerged from the bunkhouse.

"Must be a fox," one of them shouted as he checked the turkeys. "These birds is all heated up over something." The man headed for the barn to investigate.

Matthew closed the door behind him and drifted back to his bed.

Early the next morning Zack loaded Matthew onto the truck seat. Until nearly noon they drove across the fields at the base of the mesa.

Zack gestured at the fat beef cattle that grazed in the tall grass on the verdant hillside.

"Been doing pretty well this year," he told Matthew, not really hoping for a reply. He put his hand back on the wheel to control the truck on the washboard road.

"Ground's going to be too wet to use the truck out there for a while yet. . . . Only lost a few calves over the winter. . . ."

Matthew looked distractedly out across the open fields to the far horizon.

Zack stopped the truck beside a cistern set in a small grove of trees and went to the tailgate. He unloaded a big block of salt and placed it next to the water tank.

"We get these last salt licks down, we'll go in and get your dinner."

No response.

Zack got back into the truck and drove on in silence for a few minutes. He stole a sideward glance at Matthew; the boy's face was impassive.

"When you get better, I'll take you up on the mesa where we run the cattle. The air up there, so crisp it cuts like a knife. . . ."

Zack looked to see whether Matthew was listening. Matthew's face was blank.

Zack drove on.

Zack's rolltop desk was slammed open a few minutes after midnight. The room was still dark, but a slender figure moved among the furniture, searching, searching.

Matthew, his eyes wild and unfocused, frantically riffled through the desk's cubbyholes.

Through his sleep Zack heard the desk crash open and was instantly awake.

Matthew moved to the gun cabinet and started through the drawers, his fingers darting over the ammunition and cleaning swabs.

Zack appeared in the shadows at the door. "What are you doing, boy?" he asked very quietly.

Matthew looked up, panicked. He whispered frantically in a little boy's voice, "Please, please don't tell."

Zack was shocked to hear Matthew speak.

Matthew turned back to the desk, sending Zack's papers and souvenirs flying.

Zack walked up to the desk and seized Matthew's hands, spinning the boy around and dropping him into the desk chair.

"What are you talking about?" Zack demanded. "Tell who?"

Matthew was crying now, mumbling something about keys.

"Talk sense," Zack said, shaking Matthew by the shoulders. "What keys?"

Matthew began to sob. "Please don't tell Papa."

Zack stood straight with the shock of realization. He suddenly knew what Matthew was talking about.

"Matthew, that was years ago."

Matthew was desperately looking over Zack's shoulder, watching the doorway behind him. He was sure that the Reverend Mr. Hobson would appear in that doorway at any second.

"Gonna be mad at me," Matthew sobbed.

Zack put an arm around his brother and helped him up from the chair. "Nobody's mad at you. You just need some sleep, boy."

Zack led Matthew toward the door, but Matthew broke away and ran back to the desk, his fingers again searching. "But Papa . . ."

Zack sighed wearily. "Go to bed, boy. Just go to bed." Zack put his hands on Matthew's shoulders and firmly led him back to bed.

CHAPTER

Sanderson's General Merchandise was the first building anyone saw when they came into Carter from the south, an imposing brick two-story with a steeply sloped roof and high, wide porch. Inside, the dark wooden counters were piled with dry goods and cans, clothing and hand tools. The place smelled of denim, leather, grain, burlap, and machine oil.

John Sanderson, the proprietor, had gone into business late in life. He had been the first of the Sanderson clan to leave Pennsylvania in five generations. He had rolled into southern Colorado as rootless as a tumbleweed and had spent the next decade bumping from ranch to ranch, job to job, following the cattle. He boasted that for eight years he had never slept with a roof over his head or a pillow beneath it. But like Zack, he'd put aside enough money, bit by bit, to buy and build a ranch of his own.

Sanderson was soon successful in his new life, and he went back East and married his childhood sweetheart, Pleasant Ann Corbley. In 1904, the year Pleasant Ann died of influenza, he hired a foreman to run the ranch on the mesa, moved to a new house in town, and opened the General Merchandise, the most up-to-date emporium for miles around.

His daughter, Cassandra—Casey to anyone who wished to stay on her good side—ran the store, matching his capacity for hard work with her own. She had also inherited his independent spirit and his appetite for fun. And although she spent her days dutifully working behind the notions counter and keeping the store's books and the notes for the water board her father headed, her evenings were spent poring over magazine articles and books about faraway places and exotic and famous people. Next year, when she was nineteen, she planned to strike out on her own—although she hadn't worked up the courage to tell her father so.

Casey whistled as she cleaned the child-size fingerprints from the candy-counter glass. She barely looked up as Zack entered the store.

Zack listened for a minute, grinning.

" 'Whistling girls and crowing hens always come to no good ends,' " he recited.

She made a face at him and came over to the register counter, setting her feather duster down beside it.

Zack produced a shopping list from his pocket and handed it to her.

She took the list from him and ran a professional eye over it. "Cod liver oil?"

"My brother is visiting, and he hasn't been feeling too well."

Casey eyed him speculatively. "I didn't know you had a brother."

Zack took a piece of licorice from a jar on the counter and bit into it, ignoring the question. "Let me have the shares book, please."

She reached under the counter and took out the thick water board book, the ledger in which members of the irrigation cooperative recorded their shares and the dates they planned to run water into their fields. "I'll take the water day after tomorrow," Zack said as he turned to his name and wrote a date, along with "12 hours." He handed the book back to her.

"Well?" Casey demanded.

"Well, what?"

"Your brother," Casey said, exasperation in her tone.

"He's not as good-looking as me," Zack said, grinning.

Casey hit him playfully with the feather duster. "I mean, what's wrong with him?"

Zack walked across the store to a tall wooden counter and picked up a pair of jeans.

"Send along three pairs of these, and a couple of work shirts. All he has are city clothes."

He held up a pair of boots and compared one to his own foot. "These too. And we need our regular kitchen order," he said. "Flour, sugar . . . the usual. I'll have one of the men pick everything up tomorrow."

Casey wrote up a sales ticket and stuck it on a steel spike next to the register.

"You're not going to tell me, are you?" she asked.

Zack went to the door.

"Put this on the bill," he said, holding up the licorice.

"I always do," she replied to the closing door.

The next morning Zack was up before dawn, getting breakfast on the table. When the coffee was ready, he walked down the hall and opened the door of Matthew's room a crack.

Matthew was still asleep, his face to the wall and his legs drawn up nearly to his chest. Matthew slept peacefully with his blankets tucked up around his head like a protective cloak.

Zack let Matthew sleep until he had loaded the back of the wagon with tools and harnessed the team, then gently awakened him. Matthew offered neither help nor resistance as Zack dressed him, fed him a quick breakfast, and got him settled on the wagon seat.

The sun was just coming up when they reached the edge of the field. Four field hands were already there, crouched around a small cook fire near a big harrow. The men came over to greet them and offer coffee as Zack reined the horses to a stop.

Zack released the team from the wagon and led them to the harrow. One of the field hands hooked up the team while another greased the harrow's wheel hub from a can of axle grease.

Zack clucked to the team and started off across the vast field. Matthew trailed along behind.

The sky was a deep midmorning blue by the time the crew worked their way back to where the wagon was, leaving behind them a black, tumbled swath in the moist earth where the harrow had bit into it. Zack sat Matthew on the tail of the wagon while he and the other men drew water from a cask strapped to the side.

The men had slaked their thirst and were resting on the grassy hillside when Zack's foreman, George, rode up.

" 'Bout done with that lower field, Zack," George reported. "Shall we start down by the river?"

Zack shook his head. "Not yet, George. We need to get the rest of the ditches cleared; I'm running the water tomorrow night. Get on down and let me show you."

Zack helped Matthew from the wagon and took a pitchfork from the wagon bed.

"Here," he said, handing the tool to Matthew. "Time you got some exercise."

Matthew stood uncomprehendingly with the pitchfork in his hand. Zack shook his head in frustration.

"Take that thing away from him, Jorge," Zack said to one of the hands, "before he hurts himself."

The field hand walked over to Matthew, took the pitchfork, and tossed it into the wagon. Matthew simply let his arms dangle at his sides.

Zack turned to Matthew and pointed his finger. "You stay put while I talk to George. You hear?"

Matthew gave no sign that he understood, but Zack turned and walked to the edge of the ravine with George, their backs to Matthew.

On the hillside, the field hands were absorbed in their own conversation. No one was paying attention to the slender form beside the wagon.

A white cabbage moth, as large as a silver dollar, fluttered from the new-mown hay and was caught in an air current that floated it near the wagon. The movement caught Matthew's eye. He stirred distractedly.

At the gully, Zack and George were deep in discussion. They paid no attention to Matthew.

Matthew followed the cabbage moth with his eyes as the breeze carried it toward the gully. The white moth disappeared over the edge of the gully.

Zack pointed into the bottom of the dry ravine.

"Go back in and pick up the other team, and the scraper. We need to open up the ditch all along there"—he pointed to the far end of the field—"so I can get the water down here."

George nodded that he understood. "We'll get that ditch smooth as glass." He grinned.

It was only a few paces to the edge of the gully, and Matthew covered it in a matter of seconds. The rim of the ravine was broken here, and Matthew's feet were unsteady on the loose gravel as he stumbled into the ravine. Above him, just around a bend, Zack and George stood talking.

The moth skimmed the tops of wild mustard plants at the bottom of the ravine. Matthew followed, fascinated.

The ravine was six to eight feet deep and about as wide as it was deep. The gully floor, actually a dry streambed, was soft sand, grown here and there with wild mustard, prickly-pear cactus, and creosote.

The ravine walls were sheer, cut into the thin soil by years of spring flash floods. Here and there the walls were pocked with clusters of shallow erosion holes, each one about the size of a chicken-coop nest and about two feet deep. A pair of swallows darted in and out of the holes.

The cabbage moth disappeared into a creosote bush, and Matthew's eyes followed it. When the moth did not immediately emerge, the boy began to wander along the ravine, scanning the pockmarked walls but paying no attention to his footing on the uneven creek bottom.

Matthew ran his hand along the edge of a shoulder-high erosion hole. His hand touched rock, but his mind saw a cubbyhole in a big oak desk.

"I'm sorry, Papa," he mumbled. "I'm sorry."

He reached inside the hole and pulled out a clutch of dried grass. His hand reached for the next hole to the right.

Three holes away a rattlesnake withdrew deeper inside the hole in which it had sought shelter from the midday heat.

At the top of the ravine, Zack and his foreman had finalized the irrigation schedule. George was mounting his horse when Zack casually glanced back toward the wagon to check on Matthew.

"Damn!" he shouted as he ran for the wagon. "Where the hell did he go?"

Zack's shout roused the field hands on the hill to action. They ran for the wagon as Zack and the foreman reached it.

George pointed to Matthew's footprints in the dust. "That way, it looks like," he said to Zack.

Zack nodded and pointed toward the ravine. "You men fan out to the sides. I'll follow his tracks."

Zack ran toward the ravine bank.

Matthew fingered the dirt at the edge of the next erosion hole, puzzling in his mind why his mother had allowed dust to gather on his father's desk. He thrust his hand into the hole, searching.

A tiny field mouse, scared by the intrusion, scurried away along the eroded face of the wall. Matthew ignored it, intent on his task. In its fear, the mouse ran right in front of the rattlesnake's hole and scuttled into the tall grass at the base of the wall.

The snake was too startled to attack. It slowly drew its sinuous body into coils.

Matthew moved to the hole next to the one that sheltered the rattlesnake. As he rummaged inside the hole, he mumbled to himself.

His breath was coming in soft sobs now. "He's gonna make me stand up in church and tell," Matthew muttered with the voice of a six-year-old.

His hands were frantically searching the erosion hole, pulling tufts of weeds from inside and clawing the dirt floor and sides of the hole. "I'll find your keys, Papa. Don't make me stand up and tell."

The boy's movement so close to the snake's territory alarmed the deadly pit viper. It flicked its forked tongue, sensing Matthew's presence and appraising the threat. It began to rattle quietly. The rattlesnake watched Matthew with unblinking eyes.

Matthew's mind saw only the cubbyholes of his father's huge rolltop desk and his own six-year-old hands riffling through his father's papers. He heard the crisp writing paper shuffle as he searched for the lost keys.

"He's gonna make me stand up and tell," Matthew sobbed as he moved to the hole in which the snake had begun to rattle loudly. "He's gonna make me tell."

As he reached for the snake's hole, memory and nightmare combined to show Matthew the young Reverend Mr. Hobson about to slam the rolltop down on his son's small hands.

"Papa, please," he sobbed. "Please . . ."

The snake coiled tighter, ready to strike. Matthew extended his arm.

The concussion of the rifle shot filled the ravine with sound. The snake's head, hit squarely by the bullet, exploded into a lump of gore at the back of the pocket. The body, unaware yet that it was dead, writhed and twisted within the bloody hole.

At the edge of the gully, Zack lowered his rifle. The crowd of field hands, drawn by the shot, watched silently as Zack handed the gun to George and quickly climbed down into the ravine.

Matthew had not moved. His only response was to again allow his arms to dangle limp at his sides.

Zack stood a few steps from his brother, watching but unwilling to touch the withdrawn boy.

"Matthew?" Zack whispered. "Matthew? What were you doing?"

The boy gave no response. Zack took Matthew's hand and led him back to the wagon. Zack's jaw was set and determined, his face grim.

"You gotta do something about that boy," George said.

Zack nodded, not quite knowing what that something might be.

CHAPTER

The next day Zack roused George well before sunup and set the drowsy foreman to keep a wary eye on Matthew while he went into town.

Zack felt his tension begin to ease as soon as he was clear of the ranch gate; by the time he reached town, he was almost lighthearted, like a kid on the first day of summer vacation.

His spirits were also considerably improved when he stopped at the post office and found that a large package, ordered nearly four months before, had finally arrived from New York.

"Heavy," speculated Millie Krantz, the postmistress, fishing for a clue to the contents of the box. "Lot of postage there."

Zack, amused, nodded in agreement but volunteered nothing.

"Must be important to pay that much," Millie tried again.

"Just to me, Millie." Zack chuckled, tucking the box under his arm.

Millie turned back to her half-sorted mail in a huff as Zack left.

His next stop was the general store. Casey, standing on a ladder restocking the canned goods, saw him cross the street. She coyly turned her back to the door, carefully gauging her height on the ladder to leave a well-turned ankle at eye level in case Zack happened to come through the door. She managed to seem appropriately surprised when the bells above the door rang.

"Morning," she called out perkily to him.

"Morning," he replied.

She climbed down as Zack distractedly gathered up a ten-pound sack of salt, a currycomb, and a box of shoeing nails and put them all on the counter.

Casey came over to write up the sales ticket. She got the odd feeling that Zack had chosen the items at random.

"Is that all of it?" she asked.

Zack fussed with the items on the counter for a few seconds. He suddenly looked at her square, riveting her with his eyes.

"Casey, I need to find a woman," he said, his tone flat.

Casey laughed. "Finally figured that out, did you?"

"No, no." Zack blushed, flustered. "I mean to help out at my place. With my brother."

"He still not feeling up to snuff?"

"It's more than that." He hesitated. "A lot more. I really need somebody to be out there full-time." He hesitated again, then met her gaze. "Do you know anybody? I can't pay much, but . . ."

Casey put aside the order pad.

"When will you need me?"

"You?"

Casey smiled. "It can't be any worse than here. If I see another sack of black-eyed peas, I'll scream."

Zack's face darkened. "This isn't a game. You don't know what you're getting into."

"Probably not," Casey agreed.

"And what about your father? He'll have a tizzy."

"He will, won't he?" Casey said cheerfully. "Pick me up in the morning."

"The morning," Zack said absently. "It's my turn to take the water tonight," he said. "It'll have to be Friday."

Casey's willing smile brought him up short. What was he getting her into? For that matter, what had he gotten himself into?

"You're sure about this?" Zack asked. "The boy is really sick. It could be more than you bargained for."

Casey patted his hand. "Pick me up at seven."

This spirited girl might be just the person to take Matthew in hand, Zack realized.

"Seven on Friday," he echoed. He nearly danced to the door, the weight of his burden suddenly lightened because it was shared.

"Girl, I could kiss you." He winked as he went through the door.

"Promises, promises," Casey chuckled to herself.

She climbed back on the ladder with her feather duster. Then, thinking better of it, she threw her apron on the counter with gusto. She put the sign in the window, locked up, and went home to pack, whistling as she went.

The water came into Zack's ditches at midnight. Zack rode out to the main sluice and opened the gate, allowing the torrent to surge over the metal gate box and into his cleared ditch.

From then until sunup Zack and his crew hiked along the web of ditches, adjusting the flow into the various fields.

Hour after hour Zack walked the ditch banks, his shovel on his shoulder, looking for clogs or breaks in the ditch wall. Zack's rubberized boots weighed his legs down, making his calves ache and his feet feel as if they were made of lead. Matthew dozed in the back of the wagon.

By sunrise the fields were beginning to flood. The light glittered pink on the breeze-rippled water. Zack and his men were too busy to notice as they wearily slogged along the muddy dikes.

At noon Zack's fields were shallow lakes shimmering in the sun. Zack did not feel the warmth through his wet clothes as he closed the sluice gates. The crew had already started back to their quarters.

Zack trailed them to the house, leading Matthew. He dumped his muddy boots on the back porch, stripped off his soaked clothes in the kitchen, and fell face first on his bed. Matthew curled up beside him and was instantly fast asleep.

Zack awoke in late afternoon, groggy and muscle sore, to find that the hot day had turned into a balmy, still evening.

Matthew still lay quietly on the bed. Zack resisted opening the paper-wrapped package until he had washed his face and hands and changed into a clean shirt, and the chickens and Matthew had been fed. Only then did he settle Matthew into the rocking chair in the sitting room and gently pull back the brown paper wrappings of the big carton.

From inside the box wafted up the scents of pine, leather, and new paper. Buried in a nest of wood shavings were two books.

Zack picked up the top volume. "*A Connecticut Yankee in King Arthur's Court*," he said to Matthew. "I've always wanted this one; never got the chance to read it."

Matthew rocked silently in the big rocking chair.

Zack pulled out the other book, a new edition of *Huckleberry Finn*, and ran his fingers over the fine leather tooling of the spine. The creamy leather was soft under his hand. "Man has to allow himself some pleasures. . . ."

Zack carried the book to the overstuffed horsehair chair and settled in. Across the room, Matthew rocked gently in the rocking chair.

Zack began to devour *Huck Finn*. Matthew, unnoticed, began rocking more vigorously, the arc of the rocker increasing a tiny bit with each swing. His gaze was far away.

After an hour Zack laid his book aside. "I'm tuckered," he said to Matthew without looking up. "You about ready for bed, boy?"

Without warning, Matthew let out a cry of rage. He sprung to his feet and, tipping over the rocking chair, lunged at Zack.

Zack was caught completely off guard, partway out

of his chair. He feebly grappled for balance for a split second, then toppled backward.

Zack and Matthew fell to the floor.

Matthew flailed wildly with his fists as Zack scuttled across the floor, trying to get out of range.

"Matthew, calm down!" Zack yelled as he regained his feet and backed away, putting the sofa between himself and his brother.

Matthew climbed over the sofa. He windmilled his arms at Zack, backing the older brother against the wall. Zack put his arms up as a shield; Matthew pummeled against them.

"Don't do this, boy," Zack cautioned. "I don't want to hurt you."

Matthew swung erratically, out of control. Zack winced as a wild right caught him a glancing blow on the shoulder.

"Matthew, stop it," Zack shouted.

But Matthew was beyond the reach of Zack's words. He punched at Zack without eye contact, with no recognition of the target of his fury.

"Please, boy," Zack pleaded, trying in vain to shield himself from the torrent of blows. Matthew came at him again.

Zack took a deep breath and gauged his blow carefully. The massive punch caught Matthew full in the stomach, rocking him back on his feet.

Matthew doubled over. Instantly Zack went to him.

But just as Zack reached him, Matthew sprang from his crouch to butt Zack in the solar plexus with his own head. Zack was thrown to the floor; in a single lunge Matthew was on him, flailing.

They rolled across the floor, Zack trying to pin Matthew's arms to his side, Matthew fighting with adrenaline-heightened strength.

As they rolled, Zack let Matthew slither within his grasp. Working his arm under Matthew's body, he shoved his arm around Matthew's throat, choking him.

Matthew gasped for air and spun within Zack's hold. Zack managed to get his hands around Matthew's throat.

"Don't fight me," he threatened. "Stop it!"

Matthew kicked his legs, trying to hit the back of Zack's head. His madness gave him immense strength.

"Stop it!" Zack shouted. He grabbed a handful of Matthew's hair, forcing the boy's head to the floor. "Stop it!"

Matthew struggled violently beneath him. Zack thumped Matthew's head against the Oriental carpet. The boy's eyes grew wilder, but so did his thrashing.

"Stop! It! Stop! It!" Zack screamed, pounding Matthew's head against the floor, his voice a cadence for the blows. Finally Matthew began to lose consciousness.

Somewhere in his frustration and rage, Zack realized that his brother had stopped struggling. He looked down. Matthew's eyes were glazed, beginning to roll back into his head.

Horrified, Zack let go. Matthew's head thudded against the floor.

Zack gathered Matthew into his arms. The boy felt small and light.

"I'm sorry, brother," Zack mumbled, tears beginning in his eyes.

He lifted Matthew and carried him to his bed. In a few minutes Matthew stirred, focused on Zack with puzzled eyes, and rolled over in the bed.

"Sleep now, boy," Zack said softly as he left the room.

The air in the house was hot and motionless. Zack sat on the front porch in the dark until he was sure that Matthew was asleep.

Not even the trauma of the past twenty-four hours had been sufficient to prod the boy from his torpor. Everything Zack knew about his brother—his quiet ways, his inability to fight back—indicated weakness, but Zack knew Matthew was not weak. No, Matthew's gentle spirit could be a strength if Zack could get him to draw on it, to use his inner resources instead of hiding inside his own mind.

But now the problem was even more complicated. Matthew stood a good chance of injuring himself—or somebody else. Something would have to be done to contain that restless energy until Matthew could get his mind under control.

Zack stood up, stretching. He walked to the barn, falling into the familiar routine of chores as he worried at the problem. When he got the horses bedded down, he'd sit again and chew on the thing some more.

Zack entered the barn by the small side door and scooped up a bucket of oats. Deep in thought, he moved automatically to the stall where Shadrack and Meshak, his two huge plow horses, waited patiently. Zack dumped the bucket of oats into the horses' manger.

Zack affectionately scratched Shadrack's ears as the massive animal crunched the grain.

"What are we going to do about him, Shad?" Zack asked the horse. "How are we going to harness all that energy?" he asked.

Shadrack moved his head so that Zack was scratching under the halter, where he liked being scratched best.

Maybe he could send Matthew back East, Zack thought. He had heard that some doctors in New York, or maybe it was Boston, had new ideas about how to help people with troubles like Matthew's. But Zack hated the idea that Matthew would again be within his father's reach.

As Zack's mind grappled for a solution, his fingers stopped moving, and Shadrack nuzzled Zack's hand to get him to resume his scratching.

Zack smiled and patted the big horse. "OK, Shad, OK." He scratched around the edges of the halter.

Zack fingered the halter thoughtfully. The horse wasn't fond of the halter, but it gave Zack the control he needed. It was a necessary evil.

"Maybe," Zack mused, an idea forming.

The tack room had a sweetly musty smell of sawdust, well-worn leather, and horses, but the workbench was uncluttered. Zack took good care of his equipment, and the tack room showed it: Even the oil lamp's chimney was clean. Wooden pegs and shelves were attached to the clapboard walls, and on these were neatly stored currycombs and brushes, and horse and mule tack of various kinds.

Zack took a toolbox from a shelf and put it on the workbench. From the box he pulled his leather-working tools: an awl, some punches, a wooden mallet. He went to a chest of drawers against the far wall and brought back a box of small brass rivets. From a shelf under the workbench he took a pair of large sharp scissors and a hooked-end knife.

With his tools in place on the bench, Zack went to the pegs where the harnesses were stored. He took one from the wall and held it up to the light. After a few moments he put that one back and picked up another, smaller one. He moved the leather through his fingers, the strength of the material firming up his idea.

Zack carried the harness to the workbench and sat down. He picked up the scissors and began to cut.

John Sanderson was snoring loudly in his big chair, his book forgotten across his chest, when Casey came in.

"Papa?" she said softly.

Sanderson stirred, then shouldered back into the chair.

"Papa?" Casey insisted.

Her father shifted toward her and opened his eyes. "Well," he said, rubbing his eyes, "good evening, Chick." He started to snuggle back to sleep.

"Papa, wake up. I need to talk to you."

Sanderson roused himself and squared around in the chair to face her. "This sounds serious," he said with a wink.

"Papa, I've got a job," she said resolutely.

"Well, yes," he said, puzzled. "The place at the store is yours as long as you want it. You know that."

"No, Papa," she insisted. "I'm going to work for Zack Hobson."

"Hobson? Out there on the flats?" His eyes narrowed. "What doing?"

"His brother's with him. He's sick. Zack needs somebody to take care of him."

"I didn't know he had a brother."

"Well, he does, and he's sick."

Sanderson shook his head. "You're no nurse."

"Zack thinks I can do it. It's mostly just looking after things, anyway, helping out."

Sanderson saw he was losing. "For how long?" he asked.

"Zack didn't say. Until his brother's better, I guess."

Sanderson stood and went to the window, quietly looking out over his yard, his barns, his fields. All built for Casey, he thought, and now she's leaving. Well, such things happen, he reflected. She wasn't going far, he told himself, and only until the boy was better.

Then he was hit by a suspicion. "What else?" he said into the window.

Casey came over and stood beside him. "Nothing else. It's a job."

"You have a job," he said, turning to face her. "Are you in love with him? Is that it?"

"No!" Casey shouted, a bit too loudly.

"Then I don't understand."

She shrugged, her eyes averted. "They need me. Zack can't manage by himself."

"I need you here," her father said, admitting to himself that it was true.

"You can get a woman in to clean. And half the girls in town would love my place at the store. And Mrs. Hentsen will fix you a grand supper whenever you say—she's been trying to get her shoe hook into you for years." Casey giggled.

Sanderson winced at the tweak. "No, it isn't fitting," he pronounced.

"Fitting!" Casey snorted. "You're a fine one to talk about fitting. You're a fine one to talk about proprieties. When did you get such culture, Mr. Cowboy-Turned-Storekeeper?"

"You mind your language, girl," he warned.

"No, Papa. I'm needed out at Zack's, and I'm going." She flounced out of the room.

"Casey!" he called after her. "Cassandra!"

But she had locked her bedroom door behind her.

The sun was nearly up when Zack finished. He blew out the lantern and, although he was bone tired, methodically stowed his tools before walking back to the house.

Matthew was still asleep, curled into a ball at the center of the bed. Zack approached him quietly, trying not to wake the boy. Gently Zack stretched Matthew's arms, one at a time, and slipped the leather strips he had fashioned over Matthew's shoulders and around his brother's waist. Matthew did not resist as Zack fastened the cinches.

Zack eased Matthew's sleeping form so he lay parallel to the foot of the brass bed. He removed Matthew's belt and slipped it through the back of the harness, through the footboard of the bed, and back to the buckle, making a closed loop.

Matthew twisted in uneasy sleep. Zack kissed him on the forehead before he left the house.

Just after dawn Casey picked up her bags and walked quietly down the hall. She could hear her father's loud snores in the office.

She set her bags in the foyer and tiptoed into the office. The room was chilly, she noticed. Her father was uncomfortably curled into his chair, his arms wrapped around his shoulders.

Casey took a comforter from the oak chest by the door and draped it across her father's sleeping form.

She picked up her bags and went out onto the porch to wait for Zack.

Sunlight sneaked around the edges of the Navajo rugs covering Matthew's windows, but still the boy slept on. His long tangled hair fell across his eyes, making him look much younger than his years.

Matthew still wore the harness, fastened securely to the bedstead. But during the night he had managed to work his way to the floor, and now he slept in a crumpled heap beside the footboard, his head cradled against his arm.

Outside in the sunshine Zack drove the truck up to the front porch. On the truck seat beside him was Casey, wearing her good dress.

"I'll get your things," Zack said to her as he climbed down from the truck and went around to the tailgate.

George came out of the barn and walked over to the truck. "Give you a hand, boss?" he asked.

"I got it," Zack replied, picking up Casey's small suitcase. "He still asleep?" Zack asked George.

George nodded.

"I'll be back in a minute," Zack said to Casey as he went into the house.

Casey looked curiously at the house. Without waiting for Zack to return, she got out.

"Better look out for the watch turkeys, miss," George cautioned, motioning toward the end of the porch.

"The what?" Casey laughed.

George pointed at a flock of huge turkeys watching the proceedings suspiciously from around the corner of the porch.

"The watch turkeys. Boss teased 'em so they go after just about anything," George explained. "Better 'n a dog, and you can eat 'em."

He flung his hand at the turkeys and hollered, "Shoo!" The birds grudgingly moved off toward the barn.

"I'll surely keep them in mind," Casey said as she climbed the stairs to the porch. George ambled off back to the barn.

Casey wandered along the length of the veranda, touching the rocking chairs and peering into the windows. The front door was open, and she did not hesitate at the threshold as she entered.

The sitting room was silent. Casey looked around, then walked down the hall to the kitchen. She opened the door beside the pantry.

"That will be your room," Zack said from behind her.

She glanced in and saw a small bedroom, furnished in solid—if slightly masculine—Edwardian elegance. She smiled at him. "I think I'll like working here."

Zack carried her suitcase into her room and put it beside the bed. "I have to go check with my foreman. Take a look around the kitchen; I'll be back in a few minutes."

Casey heard the screened kitchen door close behind Zack.

She bounced on the bed twice: a good feather mattress. She tucked her suitcase under the bed, to unpack later. It was time to explore.

The kitchen was bright and modern: It even had its own pump, right beside the sink.

Casey opened the pantry door and found stacks of dry goods covering the shelves. Braids of onions and garlic hung from the ceiling; sacks of potatoes and flour were carefully placed on pallets to keep them dry.

The kitchen was practical, Casey thought. The blue steel stove was immense, set up to help the cookshack feed twenty men or more at roundup or harvests. Inset into the stove was a porcelain reservoir for hot water and a griddle big enough to do a dozen hotcakes at once. A marble slab was inlaid into the cabinet countertop for rolling biscuits and kneading bread.

In the center of the room was a wooden table, made by hand of smoothed timbers. A stout cast-iron meat grinder was screwed to the end of the table; beside it was a carving block with several sharp knives. For a bachelor, Zack kept a good house, Casey decided.

She entered the darkened hall, moving deeper into the house. She peeked into the dining room, stopping to admire the sideboard and the rose plates that Zack had had shipped all the way from Chicago.

Keeping an ear open for Zack's return, Casey continued down the hall. She paused at Matthew's door and tried the knob.

Inside the room Matthew moaned softly in his sleep.

Casey gently nudged the door open.

The light fell across Matthew's face, causing him to stir. He did not awaken but lay on the floor, his head still cradled by his arm, the harness holding him fast.

Casey recoiled in shock, surprise, and horror. The hallway echoed her footsteps as she ran through the length of the house, through the sitting room, and out the front door.

Zack was coming up onto the front porch when Casey burst into the sunlight.

He grabbed her arm as she ran past him. "What is it?" he demanded.

"What have you done to him?" she cried. "What have you done to that boy?"

"Calm yourself," Zack said firmly. "It's necessary."

Casey shook her head. "You've got him trussed up like an animal."

Zack tried to put his hands on her shoulders, but she shook them loose.

"He is an animal," Zack said. "An animal that has to be restrained so he doesn't hurt himself." He looked her straight in the eye. "Or you."

Casey shrank away from him. "I don't believe that."

"Believe it," Zack asserted.

"How long are you going to keep him like that?"

"I don't know, Casey," Zack said gently. "I don't know if he'll ever be really right again. But for now that"—Zack pointed toward the house with his thumb—"is the only way I can keep him alive and safe."

Casey fixed Zack with an angry eye. "I'll take care of him. That's what you hired me for. And I won't need to tie him up."

"We'll both take care of him," Zack said. "But first you have to understand what you're up against."

He took Casey's arm and led her to one of the porch rockers. She sat, not quite willingly. Zack leaned against the porch rail.

"He won't recognize you from day to day. Hell, he doesn't even recognize me."

Casey was still angry, but calming down.

"He doesn't know why he's here, or even who he is," Zack continued. "He only knows that he hurts. And he'll fight you."

Zack suddenly looked very, very tired. "I don't know if we can help him, but we have to take care of him. We're all he has."

Casey got up. "We'll see," she said as she went into the house.

Zack followed her.

Matthew didn't move as Casey entered his room. She knelt beside his sleeping form.

"Matthew?" she called softly.

Zack stopped in the doorway. "He won't answer you. You have to touch him."

Casey reached out and stroked Matthew's hair away from his eyes. As she moved her hand across his face, his eyes popped open. He recoiled in fear, scrambling as far away from her as his harness would allow. He made no sound.

Casey cried out in alarm, then turned on Zack. "Get him out of that abomination!" she demanded.

"No," Zack said.

Casey turned again to Matthew, holding out her hand. He made no move, watching her fearfully.

She turned again on Zack. "What have you done to him?" she demanded.

"This is how he's been."

Casey glanced at the cringing boy. "My God," she said under her breath.

"As a matter of fact, I suspect God had a great deal to do with it," Zack said bitterly.

Casey shot him a dirty look.

She turned again to Matthew. She got down on her hands and knees, entreating, "Matthew?"

He recoiled a little less, but he was still fearful.

"I won't hurt you, Matthew." Casey was crawling slowly toward Matthew, getting a bit closer with each soothing phrase. The boy watched her warily, his eyes filled with fear.

She was close enough to touch him now, but she sat with her hands folded in her lap, softly saying the words over and over to him as her father would talk to a skittish horse. Matthew began to rock with the rhythm.

She dared not look at Zack. Not breaking the meter, she said, "I think I'll sit with him awhile."

"You fix breakfast." Zack said. "It's time we got to it."

"He's in no condition to go with you!"

"He'll go."

Zack studied Casey and the boy for a moment, realizing she didn't understand. "We have to get some order to his mind. Maybe if we can make his body strong, give some pattern to his days . . ."

Zack unbuttoned the top button of Matthew's shirt. Casey sat down on the chair beside the bed. Zack glanced at her, waiting for her to leave.

"I need to get him dressed," Zack said. "I'll bring him out when he's ready."

Casey raised her eyebrows at him. "Why did you get me all the way out here?"

"What?" Zack asked.

"Why did you bring me out here?" Casey asked, amused.

"To help with Matthew," he said, not understanding.

"Then get out and let me do it," she said with a smile.

Zack took a step back. "I just thought, well . . . undressing him . . . you know . . ."

"I've been around men and boys all my life. I used to sneak out of piano lessons and ride up to Papa's branding camps, and I've seen the bars in town. You can't surprise me, and you can't embarrass me."

Zack blushed. "But ladies . . ."

Casey laughed. "Go, now," she said, shoving him to the door. "You hired me as a nurse. Now let me work."

Zack retreated as Casey began to unbutton Matthew's shirt. "How am I going to reach you?" she whispered. She loosened the harness and put him into a clean shirt and trousers, then sat him on the bed and knelt to tie his shoes.

Concentrating on the laces, Casey was startled to feel a warm hand touch hers.

She looked up to see Matthew's face inches from hers. His eyes were averted.

Casey's hand went to Matthew's forehead to brush his hair from his eyes. He crumpled to the floor, laying his head in her lap. She stroked his hair gently.

They were sitting like that when Zack returned, a biscuit in his hand.

"He needs both of us," Casey said simply.

Zack nodded and softly left the room. He sat at the kitchen table; down the hall he could see Matthew and Casey huddled together on the floor, a shaft of morning light haloed in her hair. She looks like some Renaissance Madonna sitting there, Zack thought.

Matthew lay with his head in her lap like a young puppy. He stared at the open doorway and did not feel Casey's tears on his face.

CHAPTER
11

An hour later George led the draft horses out of the barn and around to the front of the wagon. The huge animals shifted their weight nervously as he began to harness them, anxious to get out into the fields. George soothed them with his arm across their necks, cooing softly. It was going to be a long, busy day.

Haying season, begun in mid-May, was now into the second cutting. Two harvesting crews would be kept busy for the next three weeks; everybody on the place would work, cutting alfalfa and raking the hay with horse-drawn rigs.

Along with Zack's regular hands, extra crews would be hired to bring in the hay that was to be sold. Two men in each crew would load the cut shocks into wagons. Boys joyously out of school for the summer harvests drove the wagons up to the barns, where more men unloaded them and baled and stacked the hay.

But this was no gentle pastoral scene; it was hard, dangerous work. The men wore high leather boots against rattlesnakes. Wind and rain sometimes stopped the cutting for days at a time, so that the men worked by moonlight to keep up. The boys occasionally lost control of the spirited teams, and the men were always on the lookout for runaways.

The most dangerous job was operating the baler. A boy drove a team of horses attached to a lever to power the machine, which could pack more than one hundred bales in a day. Flakes of hay were forked on to a platform at the top of the rig, where a man stepped on the hay in the feeder to force it into the mechanism. If his timing was off, his leg was grabbed and instantly amputated.

Yet another crew would work a horse-drawn hoist contraption that stacked the bales. Meanwhile the boys raked the fields, removing stubble and pulling up the wild sunflowers by hand as they went.

Zack had brought in two old railroad cars to serve as bunkhouses for the temporary workers; when she was not at the big kitchen stove, Casey would be out in the cookshack, supervising the cooking for Zack's army. The place would buzz with strange faces and activity.

George looked at the sky, noting that the only

clouds were scattered far off to the south. Good, he thought. Maybe they'd get done in jig time this year, without fighting rain and dust storms like years past. It would sure be nice for a change.

As George finished harnessing the team, Zack came out onto the porch; Matthew stumbled along behind. "Come on, boy," Zack said matter-of-factly, tugging on Matthew's harness to hurry him.

"Morning, boss." George grinned as Zack and Matthew came up. He nodded at Matthew's harness. "New horse?"

Zack glared at him.

"Pack your gear. You're fired," Zack responded without hesitation.

George was shocked. "But, boss! I didn't mean anything by it . . ."

Zack's face was stone.

George dropped the horse tack. Zack stepped around him, as if the space George occupied was empty air, and leaned into the barn.

"Henry, get out here," Zack called.

Henry came at a run.

"Yessir?"

"You're foreman," Zack said. "Let's get at it."

Henry shot a shocked look at George, then back at Zack. George shrugged.

"Yes, sir, Mr. Hobson," Henry said.

George stomped off toward the bunkhouse. Zack ignored him.

Henry climbed up on the wagon seat as Zack sat Matthew on the wagon tail and tied the boy's harness tether off on the tailgate. Without a word, he climbed on to the seat and clucked up the horses. The wagon moved off toward the rising sun.

At midmorning Casey decided to bake bread. Rummaging through the kitchen, she realized that no one had gathered the eggs that morning. Zack had obviously expected her to do it.

She found a shallow basket in the pantry and stepped lightly from the back door into the now deserted barnyard.

The turkeys were hanging around at the end of the porch. Her whistling got their attention, and the gobbling mob came at her.

Casey stepped back onto the porch.

Casey and the turkeys warily eyed one another. The biggest tom ruffled his wings in her direction and gobbled haughtily.

That did it. Casey stomped back into the house, dropping her basket and letting the door slam behind her.

The turkeys puffed out their feathers and strutted around the bottom of the steps, victorious.

But a few seconds later the door crashed open

again, and Casey, swinging her broom at arm's length like a crusader's sword, regained her ground.

"Shoo!" she yelled, swatting at the turkeys with the broom.

Casey drove the noisy gang into their pen and slammed the gate shut behind them. The gobbling and clacking was subdued as she marched back to the house and retrieved her fallen basket.

The defeated turkeys gossiped the scandal among themselves as the girl disappeared triumphantly into the barn, whistling.

Matthew watched Casey closely all that evening, unhappy if she left the room even for a moment. Zack put him to bed soon after supper, partly to get respite from the weight of the boy's constant unspoken need. Matthew allowed Zack to strap him into the harness and went quickly to sleep.

Casey and Zack passed a pleasant evening. Casey read aloud from *Huckleberry Finn*. For most of the evening there was no conversation, only Casey reading and Zack, leaned back in his chair, eyes closed, listening contentedly.

Casey already had coffee ready the next morning when Zack came into the kitchen. He poured himself a cup, then stood and stretched. "Better get done in the barn," he said.

Casey smiled. "I'll help you as soon as I check on him," she said, going down the hallway.

She was tucking the blankets in snugly around Matthew when Zack came in quietly behind her.

"How is he?" Zack whispered.

"Asleep. He was kind of fretful when I came in, but he's settled down now."

Zack lead her out of the room.

"That's about the way it's been," Zack told her. "He has good days and bad days."

Casey brushed a wisp of hair from her eyes. She had a certain way of doing that, Zack thought to his surprise, that was, well . . .

"I'll get the pail," Casey said.

Zack shook off the thought and followed her to the kitchen.

Casey loved the warm smells of the barn as she milked: the sweet cream fragrance, the pungent straw and alfalfa mixed with grain and animal scents, all underlaid with the hot odor of the compost pile outside.

As she worked, a small barn cat came out from behind the hay bales and sat at the foot of her milking stool, watching her intently.

Zack, standing on the loft of the fodder crib above her, pitched a last flake of hay into the cow's manger, sending up a big cloud of dust.

"Are you about ready to go in?" he asked Casey.

"If you don't choke me first." She laughed, coughing from the dust.

Casey gave the udder two more tugs. Foaming streams squirted into the bucket. She directed a ribbon of the cow-warm milk at the cat.

The milk caught the cat right in the face, and she fell over backward, trying to lick the milk and get her footing at the same time. Casey and Zack laughed as the cat got up, regained her dignity, and ran off.

Casey set the milking stool outside the stall and picked up the bucket as Zack came down from the loft.

"What's this all about, Zack?" she asked. "What's wrong with him?"

Zack took the bucket from her and looked down into the foam. There were no answers there.

"Partly he's just tired," he started. "He had a hard row to hoe up at that college."

They started across the yard to the house.

"That's not all, is it?" Casey asked without looking at Zack.

Zack shook his head. "Mostly it's him and the old man."

"Your father?"

Zack nodded. "Yeah. It's been coming for a lot of years now. They butt heads every time they're together. The old man just can't let it be."

"But you said Matthew was trying to be everything your father wanted. He was a good son, the way you tell it."

"That wasn't enough, and Matthew knew it," Zack said. "I knew it too."

"Is that what it was?" Casey asked. "He wanted you both to be copies of him?"

"Not copies. Better," Zack said. "I could never do anything to suit him, so I just went my own way. But that boy tried—Lord, how he tried."

Zack opened the screen door for her, cutting off her questions with a smile.

In the kitchen Zack put the milk pail on the table while Casey set up the separator on the table. This galvanized metal contraption was about three feet tall, a nest of funnels and spouts with a long curved handle.

Zack poured the milk into the top of the separator. Casey started cranking the handle, and a flow of white milk came out of the bottom spout into the bucket positioned below. Seconds later heavy cream flowed from the top spout into a clear glass pitcher.

"From what you've said—and that isn't much—it sounds like your father's one of the most respected men in that part of the country," Casey ventured. "You said everyone looks up to him."

"Everyone but his sons," Zack said coldly. "His sanctimonious preaching about virtue. He turns virtue into a sin!"

"Zack!" Casey exclaimed, shocked. "What a way to talk about your own father."

"He wasn't a father to me, or to Matthew either. His family is that damn church. Preachers are expected to have a family down front, just like they're expected to bring their robes and hymnbook."

Casey made a minor adjustment to the separator. Zack took over the cranking, and Casey went to the stove and warmed the coffee.

"So you ran," she said as she stood there, her back to him. "You ran out on Matthew."

"I ran for my life!" Zack protested. "The pious Reverend Mr. Hobson was trying to—well, a man can take only so much," he snapped abruptly.

Casey leveled a righteous glare at him. "But Matthew must have been just a boy when you left."

"I'm not my brother's keeper," Zack snapped.

"It seems you are now," she said softly.

Zack put the cream pitcher in the icebox. Casey

helped him pour the milk into the clean bottles on the sideboard.

Zack pointed down the hall to Matthew's room. "He tried to live up to the old man's expectations. He couldn't do it." He paused a moment, reflecting. "I doubt anyone can."

Casey cleaned the separator and put it away while Zack moved the bottles into the icebox. She wiped the oilcloth table cover with her dishrag.

Without looking up at her, Zack said, "Sometimes I don't think to say thank you."

Casey, embarrassed, patted his hand. She went to the stove and brought coffee for them both.

They sat engrossed in their own thoughts. Then Zack pointed down the hall again.

"The old man pushed him, just like he pushed me. But Matthew didn't have the sense to get away."

Zack shook his head. "I think he's hiding. He's hiding from our father, and he's hiding from himself."

Zack rose from the table and slammed his fist against the icebox. "Why won't he get up on his hind legs and fight this thing?"

He averted his eyes from her. He nodded toward Matthew's room and said under his breath, "Sometimes I want to beat the living hell out of him."

Casey was angry now. "You make him sound like a

coward! He's just sick; he isn't running—like you did."

"The hell he isn't! I got on a train and rode off. He ran into his own head. Same thing."

Casey got up and went to the window. She looked out at the prairie for a long time. "There has to be another way to help him," she said finally. "We can't keep him tied up like a beast."

"You got a better idea, I'm willing to listen. Meanwhile do what I say and we just might get him through this."

Casey turned to face him. "But we have to show him love too."

"There's been enough done to him in the name of love. You'll abide by what I say, or I'll take you back into town this morning. You understand?" he asked, his voice cold.

Casey burst into tears and ran into her bedroom, slamming the door. Her sobs could be heard clearly all over the house.

Zack punched the pantry door in frustration, then knocked gently on Casey's door.

"Casey?"

No response.

"Casey?"

Still no answer.

Zack turned and went down the hall to Matthew's

room. Matthew was soundly asleep. Zack bent over and, almost timidly, kissed him and gently adjusted the harness. He sat in the rocking chair, watching the boy sleep.

More than an hour later Zack sat at his desk in the study, coffee cold in the mug beside him. He took out writing materials and began a letter.

Each morning, after Casey dressed Matthew, he would trail behind Zack into the yard as the men made ready for work. Casey would watch from her kitchen window as they became tiny figures in the distant fields. The rising sun tinted the sky with the same golds and yellows as the hay below. The prairie stretched as far as the eye could see behind them.

As she put away the breakfast dishes, Casey could see them, far away. The men were haying in the back acres now. Casey looked for Zack and spotted his crew at the crest of the low rise, far out in the fields. She could make out Zack on the bench of the wagon, driving the team slowly along, and two men loading the hay.

Several yards behind them, moving along at the same pace as the horses, came a shuffling figure who did not work but only walked quietly through the fields all day, tied behind the wagon, silhouetted against the sapphire sky.

Zack stopped at midmorning. Field hands came up the rise to take water from the barrel on the wagon. Just beyond them the huge bull grazed.

Henry rode up on horseback.

"How's old Adonis today?" Zack asked.

Henry grinned. "Knee-high grass and a hundred cows all to himself. How would you be?"

Zack grinned back; the bull looked quite content indeed.

Zack left the wagon seat and gave Matthew water from the dipper. Matthew drank without acknowledgment, focused on a point beyond the horizon.

Zack climbed back up on the wagon. He snapped up the team and moved off again. The crew fell in behind.

Zack had watched carefully for signs of improvement in the boy, but there were none.

When he had first taken Matthew from the hospital, Zack had thought that his brother would simply wake up some morning and be well again, like the hero in some fairy tale. Zack now knew that change, any change, would be gradual if at all.

Secretly, ashamed to admit it, Zack had almost begun to hope for Matthew's condition to worsen. At least then there would be movement, direction: a resolution in sight.

It seemed to Zack that Matthew's problems had always been a part of Zack's life; now that he was Matthew's guardian, he was forced to battle Matthew's demons in the boy's stead. It was an uncomfortable corner that Zack had painted himself into.

Casey too had been looking for signs of change, but her focus was on small everyday behaviors. She found it a hopeful sign that Matthew's eyes followed her around the kitchen now as she did her chores. She had experimented with meeting his gaze, expecting him to shy away or smile. But Matthew just stared at her, watching her every move until she felt an uncomfortable crawl at the back of her neck, and she would dart from the room on an invented errand.

Casey thought that the way into Matthew's mind might be to look for simple things that would touch him. She collected spring flowers for him to smell and finger. She held a currycomb in his hand, and they helped Henry groom the horses.

Once, when she was plucking a chicken for supper, a stray feather drifted across the room. She thought she saw Matthew's gaze flicker toward it for a second, so she brushed the feather against the skin of his arm. To this, as to all her other attempts, Matthew made no reaction.

"He's not ticklish," Zack said from across the table.

Casey made a face at Zack, who ignored her.

She glanced from Zack to Matthew, and back again. "He looks like you, around the eyes," she said.

"People have always said that," Zack said. "We look like our mother, both of us."

"People say I look like my mother," Casey said, tossing aside a handful of feathers. "I don't know. I can't remember her much. But I've seen some pictures, and I guess I do, a little."

"It must be awful not to be able to remember her," Zack mused. "My mother . . . well, she's a good woman."

Casey nodded. "You don't talk much about her. About your folks at all."

Zack nodded slowly. Casey, embarrassed, paid particular attention to the chicken.

"I wonder if your father is still steamed?" he finally asked.

"Most likely." Casey smiled. "But he'll get over it. He's pretty easy to come around when he knows I mean it. It will just take time."

"There's not enough time in the world for my father to come around," Zack said bitterly. He sat quietly again.

"You must miss her," Casey said, looking down at the chicken.

Zack shook his head as if shaking away a fly. "That's gone by now. I left it years ago."

"Maybe someday," Casey said soothingly.

"Maybe," Zack said, unconvinced. "I learned a long time ago not to need family."

Casey's eyes danced. "Not even one of your own?"

Her look hit Zack hard, but he lost his nerve and looked away. "Guess I haven't thought much about it," he said softly.

"Mmmmm," she said, concentrating again on her work.

As he went to wash up, Zack didn't look back or he'd have seen a twinkle in her eye. He hadn't felt this gawky since he was sixteen.

CHAPTER

Casey got up early on the morning of Matthew's birthday. By the time Zack came into the kitchen for his coffee, she was stirring the chocolate cake batter.

"Morning," he said.

"Morning," she replied, preoccupied.

"Birthday cake?" Zack asked.

Casey nodded.

"Boy still asleep? I'm going to fix this harness." Zack asked.

Casey nodded, counting the stirring strokes as Zack poured his coffee. "Twenty-five, twenty-six . . ."

"Looks good," Zack said, reaching over her shoulder and dipping his finger into the batter.

"Thirty-*one*, thirty-*two*," Casey counted, playfully nudging Zack away from the bowl.

He popped his batter-coated finger into his mouth,

grabbed his coffee cup, and headed out for the barn.

Casey floured a pan and began pouring the batter, scraping the sides of the bowl with her wooden spoon.

Suddenly there was someone beside her. She looked up and saw Matthew.

"Matthew!" She laughed. "You startled me!"

Matthew was looking intently at the batter bowl.

Casey followed his gaze. "Want a taste?" she asked.

The boy kept looking at the bowl.

Casey spooned out a bit of batter and held it to his lips. He hesitated, then opened his mouth.

Casey put the sweet batter in. Matthew closed his mouth mechanically as she withdrew the spoon.

"Good?" she asked, not really expecting an answer.

The corners of his mouth turned up in a faint smile.

Casey was shocked. "You smiled! Matthew, you smiled!" She hugged him, but he did not hug back.

Just as she released him, Zack appeared at the door, carrying Matthew's harness.

"He smiled!" She beamed.

"Let's go, boy," Zack said. He turned on his heel.

Matthew followed him wordlessly to the door. As he passed Casey, she grabbed the boy's arm. She turned to confront Zack.

"He smiled! Doesn't that mean anything to you?" she demanded.

Zack came into the room and roughly yanked Matthew's other arm, tearing him from Casey's grasp.

"He doesn't understand," Zack said.

"Doesn't he? Look at him!"

A tear had formed in the corner of Matthew's left eye.

"You're so tough," she shouted. "Nothing ever gets to you." She pointed at Matthew. "Look at him. He's not the only one bound up with that harness. You're tied together, the two of you."

"You can't always protect him," Zack hissed.

"And you can't thrash him into coming back," Casey snarled.

Zack pulled Matthew by the arm and led him outside.

Casey threw the wooden spoon at the door as it banged shut behind them.

CHAPTER

13

Mrs. Hobson had stayed close to the kitchen door all morning, surreptitiously watching for the postman.

At midmorning the Reverend Mr. Hobson had come into the kitchen for a glass of milk from the icebox and found her baking her second batch of bread of the day: "For the poor," she explained. He commended her on her industry as he retired to his study to write his sermon.

It was her husband's habit to peruse the mail before going to make his afternoon family calls. Now the time for the postman to knock—and for the Reverend Mr. Hobson to finish his sermon—were about to dangerously coincide.

Mrs. Hobson walked quietly to the door of the study. The door was ajar, and she saw the Reverend Mr. Hobson bent in deep thought over his manuscript. His desk chair creaked as he shifted his weight, settling into the work. She tiptoed away from the door.

Just as she reached the kitchen, there was a sharp rap on the door.

"Postman!" came the shout from outside.

Mrs. Hobson hurried quickly to the back door. She took the mail from the postman with a rushed smile and, as politely as possible, shut the door in the man's face.

A few seconds was all it took to shuffle through the dozen letters to find the one she wanted. It was safely tucked into her apron pocket when she unobtrusively put the rest of the mail on her husband's desk. The Reverend Mr. Hobson did not look up as she left the room.

Mrs. Hobson did not dare even to look at her prize out in the open. Her hand thrust deep in her apron pocket, she went to the pantry and stood behind the storage bins.

Hidden from easy view, she caught her breath and began to read Zack's letter. The words, spoken from behind, caught her entirely off guard.

"What have you there, Mother?" The Reverend Mr. Hobson asked, his voice booming around the small space.

Mrs. Hobson whirled around.

The Reverend Mr. Hobson stood in the pantry doorway, his hand outstretched.

Mrs. Hobson stuffed the letter back into her apron pocket.

"It's from Zachary. Matthew is better."

The Reverend Mr. Hobson still held out his hand, demanding the letter. Mrs. Hobson shrank back against the pantry shelves.

"What can it hurt? It's only a letter."

The Reverend Mr. Hobson fixed her with steely eyes. "Those two are no longer your concern."

Mrs. Hobson was shocked. " 'Those two' are my sons!"

"They turned their backs on us when they turned their backs on God," the Reverend Mr. Hobson said sternly.

"They haven't turned their backs on God or on us!" Mrs. Hobson protested. "Matthew has been ill."

The Reverend Mr. Hobson paced to within inches of his wife's face and reached into her apron pocket. She began to raise her hand to resist, but something in his face stopped her. She folded her arms across her chest.

He pulled the letter from her pocket and crumpled it into a ball. His eyes blazed as if he were delivering one of his sermons.

"Matthew has taken up with the Devil," he reproved. "I'll have no part of it—and neither will you."

The Reverend Mr. Hobson strode from the pantry to the study, Mrs. Hobson in his footsteps. He threw the crumpled letter into the fireplace.

The Reverend Mr. Hobson watched it burn for a moment, then turned again on his wife.

"That will be the end of it. Do you understand?"

Mrs. Hobson, stricken, could only watch the fire.

"Do you understand?" he demanded.

"They are your sons too," she replied quietly.

The Reverend Mr. Hobson opened his pocket watch and dispassionately checked the time.

"I need to collect my sermon notes. We must leave for home calls in ten minutes."

He snapped his watch shut with a sharp click and turned to his desk to gather his manuscript. He picked up his worn Bible and walked with dignity from the study.

Mrs. Hobson watched him go, then reached into her other apron pocket and pulled out an empty envelope. She lovingly fingered the return address. Then she turned to watch as the fire consumed the last of Zack's letter.

There had been no seasons inside the asylum, but the sanctuary to which Zack took Matthew was drawn and defined by the outdoors. The weather in southeastern Colorado is big and changeable. A bright morning can, in a few hours, become a dark afternoon of violent thunderstorms and gale-force winds.

Thunderstorms at the eastern foot of the Rockies are dangerous in several ways. Lightning strikes illuminate the sky for hours, randomly setting fires. But perhaps more dangerous is the rain such storms bring. On the prairie the sky can still be blue; but all the while, hidden from the flatlanders, the rain dropped high in the range rushes down the canyons in a wall of water, erasing everything in its path. Such storms cut deep chasms in usually dry creek beds and carry off roads, livestock, or buildings without warning.

People who live on the land of the eastern slope learn to watch the mountains. Rain is viewed with mixed feelings: relief mingled with caution.

Zack had seen the damage that the storms could do. In late summer he spent several weeks shoring up the irrigation ditches and clearing creek beds of underbrush and weeds, all the time keeping an eye on the skies.

The cluster of white clouds over the mountains that morning concerned Zack, but there were still two creeks to clear. The morning had been beautifully warm, but by late afternoon, thunderheads were glowering over the stubbled fields. A brisk, hot wind came up from the south as the afternoon light became crisp yellow.

Matthew leaned against the wagon tail, watching the clouds and humming softly to himself, while four hands cleared the irrigation ditch a few feet from him. Zack worked beside them, sweat soaking his shirt and hatband.

A flash of lightning ripped from the clouds to the top of the mesa. Zack looked up, counting for the thunder. Four seconds later it came, shaking the air as it rolled across the fields.

"Close," Zack said. "We'd better get in."

He threw his shovel into the back of the wagon.

"Henry, you get that team turned around," he shouted. "Stow those shovels," he yelled to the men. "We don't want to get caught out in the open like this."

The men threw their tools into the wagon and climbed aboard. Zack shoved Matthew into the back of the wagon.

As Henry clucked up the team, there was another lightning bolt, closer than the first. Zack instinctively wrenched his head toward it and saw a wall of rain coming along the foot of the hills toward them.

"We've got to get on higher ground," Zack yelled. "The flash floods'll be coming down."

Henry lashed the team into a gallop, and they rattled across the fields toward the house. The boy lowered his head and shivered as the rain poured down on them.

Casey looked out the window. The sky above the barn was filled with towering black clouds. The temperature outside had dropped twenty degrees in as many minutes. Rain and lightning curtained her view of the hills. Casey jumped and hugged her arms as thunder rocked the kitchen.

Zack shoved the door open and burst into the kitchen, pushing Matthew ahead of him. Matthew was shivering. Casey ran to help.

"Get some blankets," Zack barked through his own chattering teeth. "He's drenched."

"Coffee's hot," Casey called over her shoulder as she went to the closet.

Zack pushed Matthew into a chair and poured him a cup of coffee. He wrapped Matthew's fingers around the cup, and the boy grasped the warmth with both hands, still shaking.

"Miserable out there," Casey said as she came back with an armload of blankets.

Zack nodded as the kitchen filled with blue light and another clap of thunder rocked the room.

"That was close by," she said.

Matthew had dropped his coffee. He was trembling with fear.

Zack nodded at the boy. "Let's get him to bed."

Together they helped Matthew to his feet and led him to the bedroom. Zack got the harness off, struggling to get the soaked leather through the buckles. It took both of them to peel off Matthew's wet clothes.

Casey turned down the bed as Zack began to dress Matthew. She handed Zack a clean nightshirt.

"No, just get me a clean pair of trousers and a soft shirt," Zack said, handing the nightshirt back. "I can't put the harness over that."

"You're not going to tie him in that tonight?" Casey said, incredulous. "Look at him!"

Zack was stern. "He's strong as three men when he gets upset. You going to hold him down?"

The steamer trunk sat open beside the bed, where Casey had been unpacking it; Matthew's clothes were spilled out and a tennis racket and old fiddle case was tossed on top. She grabbed a shirt and pants.

Casey helped Zack put Matthew into the dry clothes. She reluctantly watched as Zack put the harness back on, buckling it tight around Matthew's back and waist.

A flash of light showed at the edges of the Navajo rugs hung against the windows, and instantly there was another roll of thunder. Matthew, terrified, cringed and fell down on his bed in a fetal position, his eyes wild.

Casey rushed to him and cradled him. "Matthew? It's OK, Matthew . . ."

"Angry," Matthew whispered.

Casey and Zack looked at each other.

"Angry," Matthew said again.

"Who's angry, Matthew?" Casey urged, stroking his hair.

Matthew snuggled closer to her. "God," he whispered fearfully.

Zack quickly attached the harness to the bedpost. "Damn storm. Scaring the boy out of his mind."

Casey held Matthew close.

"God isn't mad at you, Matthew. It's just a thunderstorm. It'll pass."

Matthew was sobbing with fear even as Casey cradled him. She framed his face with her hands, trying to make him focus on her.

"Listen to me, Matthew," she crooned. "Do you know what a thunderstorm is?"

Matthew only stared at her, wide-eyed.

"My papa used to say it was just the sound of the angels laughing," Casey said, trying to keep her tone light. "That's all."

Zack snorted, rolling his eyes.

"Shush now," Casey shot at him, annoyed.

She cradled Matthew closer. "Don't be afraid, Matthew. It's a happy sound, up in the sky. You know, 'Make a joyful noise.' "

She began to rock him in her arms. Matthew relaxed a little. Casey started to hum tuneless notes to comfort him.

"He needs to rest," Zack said. This bonding between Casey and his brother made him uncomfortable, as if he should be a part of it but couldn't understand how. Feeling shut out, he turned on his heel and left the room.

Casey snuggled Matthew one more time, then tucked the covers in around him and went to the door. Matthew rolled himself tighter, his knees as far up under his chin as the harness would allow.

"Come on out and let the boy sleep," Zack commanded from the other room.

As Casey closed the door, a huge white light framed the edges of the Navajo rugs in the windows and another thunderclap possessed the room.

In the silver-gray hours of the morning Zack woke up. He had folded back the Navajo blankets before he went to bed to let the breeze cool the house, and the full moon filled his window.

At first he could not understand what had awakened him. Then a few faltering notes of "Amazing Grace" resonated through the adobe.

Zack was on his feet in five seconds, and at the door of Matthew's room in five more.

He hadn't imagined it. Music—fiddle music—was coming from Matthew's room. Casey. It must be Casey, he thought, trying to snap Matthew out of his stupor. He'd put a stop to this once and for all . . .

But as he reached for the doorknob, he heard Casey's door open at the far end of the house. Then Casey was standing beside him at Matthew's door, her robe askew and her hair falling out of the braid in which she had plaited it for bed.

They exchanged looks that passed for questions, but neither had answers. Zack carefully pushed Matthew's door open.

Matthew was seated cross-legged on the floor, wedged between the bed and the trunk. On the floor beside him was his open fiddle case; his fiddle was cradled under his chin. As Zack opened the door, Matthew drew his bow across the strings again.

"Amazing Grace" began again, stronger and more sure. Matthew's eyes were closed, but his face bore the first peace Zack had seen there.

Zack tiptoed into the room and sat on the floor, facing his brother. Matthew opened his eyes.

"Joyful noise," Matthew murmured, his voice wispy and thin from disuse.

Zack jumped. "What?"

"Joyful noise," Matthew said, insistent. The fiddle was louder, more confident.

Casey, standing in the doorway, caught on first. "Make a joyful noise," she said.

Matthew nodded, his eyes dreamy. He swayed in time with the music he was making.

Zack finally understood. He hugged Matthew, and Matthew did not recoil.

"Yes, Matthew. Make a joyful noise." The tears were streaming down Casey's face, and Zack's too.

Matthew's breath was coming in deep sobs. "Music is mine?"

"Of course, boy."

"He can't make me . . ." His voice trailed off.

"No, boy, he can't take it," Zack said, his voice hard.

"Music is mine," Matthew said determinedly.

He began to play again, a faint smile starting among the subsiding sobs.

"Be happy, Matthew," Zack said. "Make a joyful noise."

Zack sat quietly beside Matthew while the boy played on and on until falling asleep in his brother's arms.

CHAPTER

Matthew slept for three days. Casey worried, but Zack urged her to let the boy sleep, noticing that Matthew no longer tossed fretfully in the bed or writhed in nightmares.

When Matthew finally awoke, he was disoriented and sheepish, his voice raspy. But over the next weeks he began to respond, a little at a time. The morning Matthew asked Casey if he could have an apple with his breakfast, Zack knew the boy was on his way back.

A few days later Matthew began to show his first interest in the work on the ranch. Zack left him at the wagon while he started a crew on a new ditch. When he came back, he discovered that Matthew had picked up a shovel and made a few tentative scrapings at the ditch bank.

Zack rigged a long tether for Matthew's harness to allow him greater freedom. As the summer went on, Matthew was working more and more alongside the ranch crew. In the evenings he sat on the porch with the rest and shucked corn, content to listen and busy his hands with the repetitious work as the others laughed and gossiped.

By autumn Matthew's arms had become strong, his stomach hard and flat, and his legs muscled out. His speech had also improved, which Zack took as a sign that his mind was becoming more whole. At first he tried to communicate with them by a combination of gestures, pointing, and halting words. Before long he was able to say complete sentences, although never with eye contact.

One morning, as they were driving to town in the truck, Matthew called out, "Stop!"

Zack hit the brakes, not knowing what the problem was. Matthew pointed into the pasture.

"Adonis?" Matthew asked.

"Sure is," Zack said proudly.

"Sure is something," Matthew said.

"He's half yours, remember?" Zack said, ruffling Matthew's hair.

Matthew looked at him with wonder. "For real and true?"

"For real and true," Zack repeated.

"Well, that's something," Matthew said, satisfied.

That afternoon Matthew followed Zack into the barn. Zack sat Matthew on a hay bale, picked up a pitchfork, and started cleaning out the stalls. Matthew watched him intently.

"Want to help?" Zack asked.

Matthew nodded. Zack handed him a pitchfork, and together they finished the job.

Zack watched Matthew spread fresh hay in the last stall. The boy was working evenly and diligently.

"Come out here a minute," Zack said, tapping Matthew on the shoulder.

Matthew followed him out of the stall and sat on a hay bale. Zack sat on another bale opposite him.

"You all right, boy?" Zack asked.

"I feel fine. Just a little tired, that's all."

"No," said Zack. "I mean the other."

It was a long time before Matthew spoke.

"It makes me sad he'd do that to me," he finally said.

It was Zack's turn to nod. "You have to take hold of it for yourself, Matthew."

Matthew nodded that he understood.

Zack took a long look at his brother, then stepped behind him and unbuckled the harness.

"You sure?" Matthew said apprehensively.

"You'll be fine."

Matthew got out of the harness. Zack picked it up and carried it into the tack room.

Matthew went back to work in the stall. Zack winked at him as he walked back to the house, leaving the boy alone in the barn.

Behind him he could hear Matthew whistling a hymn under his breath.

After the Sunday noon meal, Zack put on his irrigation boots and rode out to Peter Mooney's place, three miles to the east, for the water board meeting.

Zack had been talked into serving on the water board because his place backed up to the main ditch on two sides. The ditch companies were owned by the landowners, each holding enough water shares to supply his own needs. For each share, the holder was obligated to keep his own ditches clear and to supply men to work the bigger channels of the system. It required plenty of manpower to keep the ditches running.

Board members also took their turns riding the ditch system to prevent anyone from diverting too much water at one time. One popular way of stealing water was easy: Just put a board across the main flow, and the water surged over into the wrong field. More subtle thieves used branches and debris to make it look like a natural clog.

Without the water the valley would brown and die. The ditches were the arteries that bound the farms and ranches together, and they were jealously guarded. Board members took their duties seriously, and each month they met at a member's sluice box to see first-hand that all was well.

Zack cut over to the river road, taking his time and enjoying the shade from the big trees that overhung the banks. The peace and quiet soothed him.

Eventually he reached Mooney's fence line, and in the distance Zack could see four men on horse-back waiting at Mooney's sluice box. He recognized Mooney and the two ranchers from down east. The man on the big bay was Casey's father.

Damn, Zack thought. He'd forgotten that Sanderson would be there. Well, tough it out.

He rode up and extended his hand to the other board members. Sanderson only nodded solemnly and said "Hobson" in recognition as Zack shook his hand. There was no clue as to what the man was thinking.

The board meeting was informal and quick, carried on as the men rode the ditches. They worked their way back toward town along the main ditch, stopping occasionally to inspect a dam or sluice box, or to make notes in the water ledger that Sanderson carried.

When they reached the river road, Zack waved good-bye and started to turn off.

"A minute, Hobson," Sanderson said behind him.

Zack turned and saw that the others were already far down the road, leaving him alone with Sanderson at the crossroads.

"How is your brother?" Sanderson asked evenly.

"Better, sir," Zack said to the older man. He wasn't going to say any more than he needed to until he knew which way the wind was blowing.

Sanderson nodded. There was much in Zack that he recognized in himself: a certain independence, a strength, a toughness of will. And a stubbornness.

"And Cassandra?"

"She's been a great help, sir. I couldn't have managed without her."

Sanderson nodded again. "So she'll be coming home soon?"

Zack didn't blink. "I don't know for sure. My brother still needs attention. He's had a rough time of it."

Sanderson considered. "Well, give her my love." He

reined his horse around and kicked it to catch up with Mooney and the others.

It was almost a blessing. At least it was a concession of Casey's right to make up her own mind. Zack, relieved, watched him go, then turned toward the river road, his head buzzing.

Matthew was better, it was true. So why was he telling Sanderson that Casey was still needed?

He suspected he knew the answer: that it wasn't just Matthew who needed her now.

The night sky out on the edge of the Rockies is brittle and deep, like black ice on a winter lake. Stars punch through in glittering bursts. Hazes of stars too far away to see individually curtain the bright constellations; shooting stars add pyrotechnics. The dome is high and wide, and movement is everywhere.

Zack and Casey sat in the porch rockers, savoring the last of the lazy autumn evenings.

There was a muffled crash from Zack's study. Zack turned his head toward the door and started to get up. Casey lightly touched his hand and shook her head, and he settled back into his chair.

"He's working on the letter," Zack said.

"Not making much headway, I'm afraid," Casey replied.

"This is the third night he's been at it," Zack said.

"Would you know how to begin?" Casey asked, looking over her shoulder at the lighted office window.

In the office Matthew righted the wastebasket he'd kicked over.

He sat at the desk, holding a pen but staring off into space.

After a few seconds he threw down the pen and leaned back in his chair, disgusted. He paced up and down the office a few minutes, hands thrust into his pockets.

An idea came to him; he lunged at the desk and scribbled a few lines.

No good. He set his jaw and crossed the lines out, then gouged a few more sentences into the paper.

He read them, then tore it up. He banged his chair back so hard that it fell over as he stood to pace again.

On the porch it was Zack's turn to caution Casey back into her chair.

"He'll get it done." Zack shrugged. "He has to do this himself."

They could hear Matthew inside storming around, banging furniture.

"If he doesn't tear your house down first." Casey

grinned as she sat back. "He really is better, isn't he?" she asked.

"Seems to be," Zack said.

Casey was quiet for a long moment, then pulled her shawl more snug around her shoulders.

"I suppose I should be moving back into town, then," she said.

Zack studied his boots for a long time before he said anything.

"We need you here," he finally said quietly.

"You just told me he was better," she said.

They were both looking at points far off in space as they talked, neither daring to look at the other.

"All right. I need you here," Zack said. He extended his hand to Casey.

She smiled and took it without looking at him. They sat and rocked, hand in hand, and silently watched the shooting stars.

Elizabeth Hobson modestly turned the light low as she dressed for services, valuing a few moments alone while the Reverend Mr. Hobson collected his sermon notes. Laying her cotton housedress on the bed, she washed up with her rose water, the one vanity she permitted herself, from the basin on the washstand. She dusted her throat and arms with a puff of unscented talc before putting on her best dress, a heavy dark-green silk with black braid at the high collar, sleeves, and fitted bodice. She carefully secured her best pearls around her throat; her husband was proud of them, thinking them a fitting and demure decoration for a preacher's wife. She thoughtfully twisted the sapphire ring back onto her finger.

Mrs. Hobson tidied up the room a bit when she had finished dressing, trimming the lamp and straightening the quilt on the bed. As she picked up her house-dress to place it in the hamper, she felt the stiff corner of Zack's envelope in the pocket.

She jumped, feeling like a child caught being naughty.

Glancing around the room, she looked for a safe hiding place. She was unsure of the Reverend Mr. Hobson's reaction if he found it—and she had no wish to find out.

She went to the bed stand. His Bible lay on the table, close to the edge of the bed. She opened the drawer and saw a scattering of pencils and fountain pens, along with scraps of paper. If her husband awoke in the night, it was to write notes for a sermon, and he wanted writing materials at hand. Not a safe hiding place for Zack's envelope, she realized.

It occurred to her how little of the room, of the

house, was really hers. The bed stand with his pens and sermon notes; the nightstand with his shaving kit beside the washbowl; the tall cedar-lined chifforobe, its doors standing open to reveal his frock coats beside her other two good dresses. Even the kitchen was run and organized according to his needs and specifications.

The bureau? She opened her handkerchief drawer and removed a fresh white square, embroidered with the monogram *E*. Her husband, uncomfortable with seeing her personal linen ("things of the flesh," he called them), was unlikely to open any drawer in which she stored her clothing, but she couldn't take the chance.

No, the safest place, she finally realized, was on her person. The Reverend Mr. Hobson would have little chance of discovering the envelope if she kept it with her at all times.

She tucked the envelope in the bodice of her dress near her heart and went downstairs to get the girls ready for church.

The Reverend Mr. Hobson confidently began the service with the opening prayers, the announcements, and the reports of home visits. He started warming to his subject as he worked his way through the scripture text, and by the time he reached midsermon, he was in high form.

"... and from Jeremiah we read, 'Why, then, is this people of Jerusalem slidden back by a perpetual backsliding?' "

In the third pew a small boy squirmed, trying to touch the shiny brown pebble he had secreted in his pocket. The preacher fixed the boy with an unblinking eye. The boy snuggled up to his mother.

" 'They hold fast deceit; they refuse to return . . .' "

In the front pew the preacher's wife was barely listening. She absently fingered the bodice pocket of her dress, reassuring herself that the envelope was there.

In the pulpit the Reverend Mr. Hobson was winding up for his dramatic finish.

"Backsliding!" He paused for effect. "Now there's a familiar road!"

He picked up his Bible, holding it out in front of him as if it was a talisman to ward off evil spirits.

" 'I hearkened and heard,' " he read aloud, " 'but they spake not aright. No man repented of his wickedness, saying "what have I done?" Every one turned to his course, as the horse rusheth into battle.' "

The Reverend Mr. Hobson closed his Bible and bowed his head, sorrowing. "No man repented," he said very quietly.

There was silence in the big church. The preacher's hand crashed down on the pulpit.

"*No man repented!*" he shouted. In the fifth row an elderly man started awake.

The Reverend Mr. Hobson shook his Bible at the congregation.

"*No man repented,*" he yelled at them. "It is the same today. Three thousand years, and still we are asked."

He set the Bible aside and brought both fists down on the pulpit with an echoing crash.

"Repent!"

His face was reddening now with exertion.

"Repent, for the fires of . . ."

He began the downswing for another blow but diverted the motion to the sides of his head. Clutching his temples, he slumped against the side of the pulpit.

Mrs. Hobson, suddenly brought out of her reverie, rose from her seat. She was immobile, her handkerchief pressed tightly to her mouth.

The Reverend Mr. Hobson was gripping the rim of the pulpit to support himself. His face was even darker red, his mouth still working to form the word *Repent*, though no sound came out.

His legs folded under him; as he fell, his hand knocked his Bible to the floor.

The sound of the book hitting the hardwood floor was like a cannon shot. The church exploded in action. The choirmaster and deacons lunged toward the pulpit as the occupants of the first five or six rows of pews crowded around the fallen preacher.

As the congregation surged forward, Mrs. Hobson stood in her pew, unable to leave her place.

"Somebody help him. God help him," she sobbed as the crowd closed him off from her view.

Casey dried the last of the supper dishes and looked out the window, throwing the dishrag over her shoulder. The turkeys were setting up a ruckus.

Roscoe Parnesduff, fourteen and gawky as the birds, was standing at the bottom of the porch stairs, bracing his Western Union bicycle between himself and the turkeys.

Casey put a dime in her pocket and stepped out on the back porch, ready to defend against the marauding fowl. But the turkeys scattered as Roscoe dropped his bike and scampered up the stairs.

"Evening, Roscoe," Casey said. "What brings you all the way out here so late?"

Roscoe took a telegram from his hatband and handed it to her. "Evening, Miss Casey. Mr. Carmichael sent me to fetch this to you."

Casey took the telegram, her alarm growing.

"Must be important for him to send you all the way out here on your wheel, it getting dark."

Roscoe shifted uncomfortably from one foot to the other. "I gotta get back to town, ma'am."

Casey reached into her skirt pocket and pulled out a dime. She handed it to Roscoe.

Roscoe drew back from her hand. "Oh, no, ma'am. I couldn't. Not this time." He turned and nearly ran back down the steps to his bike. " 'Bye, ma'am. Sorry, ma'am," he called over his shoulder as he made for the road.

Casey looked down at the telegram as if it had just turned into a deadly snake in her hand.

It was addressed to Zack. Casey tore it open, her heart ringing in her ears.

Zack wiped his sweaty palms on the sides of his pants and walked into Sanderson's General Merchandise.

Matty Phillips, one of Casey's friends, was behind the counter. Zack gave his order to Matty and started loading supplies into the truck. As he carried a flour sack across the board porch, his eye was caught by a patch of greenery at the far end. He put the flour sack in the truck bed and went to investigate.

Trees. Sanderson apparently had ordered bare-root

trees from back East. There were fruit trees here, and even a few willows.

Zack thought about the cool shade along the river. It would be nice to have shade like that up near the house. He fingered the burlap that bound the willow's roots.

"They make a nice canopy," said a voice behind him.

Zack turned to find John Sanderson standing close behind him. Zack instinctively took a step backward.

"Nice trees. Just got 'em in," Sanderson said.

Zack agreed. "I was thinking the willow would cast a nice shade over my side door."

Sanderson nodded. "You don't want to put 'em down too close to your well. Roots'll be all in the shoring. But up near the house should be all right." Sanderson paused. "You thinking about adding on to your place?"

Zack nodded in return. The man ought to just ask about her outright, Zack thought. "I guess I'll take it," Zack said, holding up the tree.

Sanderson considered for a moment, then seemed to have made up his mind. "You tell her it's from me. Ought to shade her kitchen window nice while she does up the dishes."

Zack, greatly relieved, offered Sanderson his hand. "Thanks. I'll tell her."

Sanderson shook his hand firmly, then went inside without another word.

Casey stood at the sink window, watching. The kitchen was darkened, although it was well past the hour to light the lamps.

Outside she could see Zack return in the wagon and pull up to the barn.

Casey slipped out the back door. Zack was unloading the rest of the supplies as she walked up to him.

"Evening, missy," he said, smiling. Then he noticed the look on her face.

"What is it?"

"Your father," she whispered. She took the telegram from her apron pocket and handed it to him.

Zack read it quickly. "He's had a stroke," Zack said.

Matthew emerged from the barn behind him.

"Father?" he asked, his voice husky with unidentifiable emotions.

Casey looked miserably from Zack to Matthew, then back again.

"Your mother wants you both to come home," said Casey.

"If we pack now, we can leave on the first train in the morning for Denver," Zack said. He took Casey's arm and started for the house.

Matthew lingered by the barn door.

"I can't," he rasped.

Casey and Zack exchanged looks as Zack turned to the boy.

"Mother needs you there," Zack said firmly.

"I won't be any help to her," Matthew said, shrinking against the barn door. "You go."

"And what about him?" Zack asked.

"I can't," Matthew said simply. He took a dirty envelope from his pocket and handed it to Zack. "Give him this."

Matthew walked off into the field. Zack stalked into the house.

Casey stood in the middle of the yard, watching them both go.

Zack refused to let Casey come to the station. She followed him to the truck, holding his left hand while he carried his carpetbag in his right.

"Where is he?" Zack asked.

Casey nodded toward the barn loft. "He's been up there most of the night."

They walked silently together across the yard to the truck. Henry sat at the wheel.

"You sure you can't get him to come with me?" Zack asked.

Casey shook her head. There were a hundred things she wanted to say—but not in front of Henry.

Instead she said, "Better go. You'll miss your train."

Zack turned to her, worry in his eyes.

She kissed him on the cheek. "I'll take care of him," she whispered.

Zack climbed into the truck. "I'll be back as soon as I can."

Casey nodded, glancing toward the silent barn. "We'll be fine."

Zack motioned toward the road, and Henry pulled away. Zack glanced up at the barn as they drove past, but no one could be seen.

Casey walked back to the porch. As she passed the kitchen steps, she stroked the bare branches of the willow tree Zack had planted. Just a stalk now, she mused, but it would grow. She was pleased at the gift, and the promise it implied.

She slumped into the rocker, studying her fingernails. Her hands looked terrible, the result of caring for the house and for Matthew.

The boy still had not let it out, she worried. What if he had a relapse? Suddenly she was exhausted.

From the barn came the first few soft notes of an old hymn, played without feeling on a fiddle.

The parsonage had been overflowing with people all day. Mrs. Hobson greeted them herself, feeling that it was her duty to comfort her husband's friends and parishioners as he would have done.

But by late afternoon the strain had begun to tell on her. Her sister Agnes had finally persuaded her to go upstairs and lie down for a bit, and Elizabeth had to admit that she felt somewhat better for the rest. Each day had now become a series of small accomplishments at holding her composure: just until noon, just until afternoon callers had gone, just until she could steal away for a nap, just until supper.

Of course the girls weren't old enough to be of help, Elizabeth mused. They were barely old enough to understand what had happened, the dear lambs. Mary Margaret, almost nine now, had assumed a self-important air and insisted on being the center of attention, not quite comprehending the reason for the uproar. And Amy, now seven, was confused and bewildered by the never-ending parade of somber people through her home.

Elizabeth, coming downstairs from her nap, heard yet another knock at the door. Her neighbors were setting up a potluck supper in the dining room, and they all seemed to have their hands full. Elizabeth sighed, smoothed her black crepe dress, and opened the door.

Framed in the doorway was Zack, his bag on the ground at his side and his hat in hand.

"Hello, Mother," he said softly. "How is Father?"

For the first time since her husband's death, Elizabeth Hobson began to cry.

At ten the parsonage was still filled with people talking in hushed tones, the sideboards still laden with food brought for the family. Zack and his mother moved to the front door, hoping that people would get the hint.

Brother Willows's wife, Abigail, noticed and realized it was time to go. She nudged her husband and gathered up their wraps. Others saw them preparing to leave and followed them to the door.

"Thank you for coming . . ." Zack started, groping for the name.

"Brother Willows, Abigail," his mother finished for him, taking the guests by the hand.

"He will be deeply missed," Brother Willows said. Mrs. Willows nodded solemnly.

Elizabeth shook hands with them again, then turned to the couple behind them. The Willowses found themselves to have been warmly and skillfully nudged out the door.

Fifteen minutes later the house was emptied, the last few women to leave protesting politely that they should stay and help clean up, Elizabeth just as politely replying that it could wait until morning.

As the last parishioners pulled away from the house, Zack closed the door and put his arm around his mother's shoulder.

"Are you sure you won't reconsider?"

"Zachary," she said firmly, "I have my own life here. My friends, your father's work . . ."

"Matthew and I both want you to come. I don't much like the idea of your being alone."

Elizabeth shook her head. "Your father left us well provided for, and I have your aunt Agnes close by. The girls and I will be fine."

They sat on the parlor sofa. Elizabeth pointed around the room.

"Zack, look around you. This is my home. You just take care of Matthew."

Zack took her hand. "Matthew is finally learning to take care of himself, I think."

She kissed him absently on the cheek.

"He loved you both, you know."

Zack patted her hand fondly but said nothing.

That same evening, a thousand miles to the west, Matthew sat in one of the rocking chairs on Zack's front porch and looked off into the fading light. His fiddle case rested across his knees; he stroked it absently for comfort.

Casey came out the side door. She dumped a pan of water into the moat around the tiny tree.

She went up onto the porch and settled into a chair beside Matthew. She watched him squirm miserably in his seat, unable to get comfortable.

"Are you all right?" she asked.

"I just keep thinking how he did this to me," Matthew said. "I can't feel any charity for him now he's sick."

"Because he wouldn't answer your letters?"

"Because he refused to see how unhappy I was."

Casey shook her head. "He thought he knew what was best for you. He was your father."

Matthew's fingers caressed the fiddle case.

"That fiddle is very important to you, isn't it?" Casey asked.

Matthew shrugged. "I guess so."

"Why?" Casey prodded.

"I don't know," Matthew said after a moment's hesitation.

Casey looked at him sternly. She'd caught him in a lie.

Matthew averted his eyes.

"He bought it from a fiddler to stop some barn dances," Matthew began, pronouncing *He* as a name of great power. "I guess I wanted it because he tried to destroy it. He only saw the sin in it . . ."

Matthew sighed and got up. He wandered toward the barn, carrying the fiddle case.

Inside the barn, Matthew tucked the fiddle case under his arm and climbed into the hayloft. There he sat cross-legged, the case open in front of him. He inhaled the sweet ripe hay smells, the pungent animal scents mixed with a high hint of ammonia wafting from the manure. The loft smelled warm and dark and safe.

The images were there with him. The night he stole down the stairs and rescued the fiddle from the wood-pile. The look on the dean's face as he expelled him. His father's eyes. Sounds too: snatches of hymns from school and from his father's church, catchy tunes Cappy used to hum, and the sounds of trains.

Matthew drew his bow across the strings to silence the other sounds. The clear cleansing tone vibrated low from the instrument.

Matthew played another, and one more, not caring if a song was there or not. It was the sound itself, the sound he made of his own bidding, that could heal him.

He closed his eyes. The music carried him up.

Finally there were tears.

Casey, still sitting on the porch, heard Matthew begin the hymn she had heard him play so often. But this time, it was different. There was mood and feeling there, a personal intonation she had never heard before in Matthew's playing. "Please," she prayed silently and to no one in particular.

Then it was quiet, too quiet. Casey stayed in her chair for as long as she could, the silence stretching out and becoming unbearable. What was he doing up there, all alone?

Casey rose from her seat. She took a step toward the barn. Should she invade his privacy? She sat down again.

But what if he had had another of his "spells"? She had half-risen from the rocker when there suddenly were fiddle notes again from the barn.

But now the music had changed. Matthew was playing slowly and dramatically, the fiddle resounding with deep, mellow notes. At first Casey didn't recognize the tune.

Then she realized that Matthew was playing that dance tune "Fiddler's Joy," but so slow it sounded like a mournful ballad. All the emotion, the rage and sorrow, that had been bottled up in Matthew was coming out through the music.

Casey's eye caught a glint in the sky. She looked up as a meteor flashed near the Big Dipper. She wished on it, tears touching her eyes.

The music was changing again as Matthew's raw

emotion began to ebb. The music was setting him free.

Casey heard the tempo rise from the barn as "Fiddler's Joy" became a sprightly dance tune, just as the fiddler had played it. Casey knew that Matthew was imprisoned no more.

The Brookbend Protestant cemetery was large, with great oak trees and a manicured lawn beneath the impressive monuments. Here and there, behind elaborate wrought-iron fences, were private mausoleums.

The grave of the Reverend Mr. Andrew Hobson was entirely covered with sprays, floral crosses, and wreaths of flowers bedecked with gold lettering on satin ribbons: *Beloved Husband, Faithful Pastor.* Surrounding it was a backdrop of even more flowers in baskets and urns, brought from the funeral parlor. Added to these were personal bouquets brought by parishioners who even now, two days after the services, still sporadically filed through the huge cemetery gates to pay their respects.

It was early evening, and in the twilight the flowers still looked fresh. Their fragrance, green and cinnamon-sweet, wafted up to Zack, alone beside the grave.

Zack wore his traveling clothes and his good Stetson. His carpetbag rested on the ground beside him.

After a moment Zack removed his hat. There was no sorrow in his expression, but there was regret.

He removed Matthew's sealed letter from his pocket. Zack slid it in among the flowers.

He stood a few more moments, hat in hand. Then he picked up his carpetbag, put his hat on, and walked resolutely away from the grave without looking back.

CHAPTER

Two weeks later Matthew stood alone at dusk on the train platform in Carter, watching down the tracks to the east.

There was still a glow on the horizon; another bad storm had passed through earlier in the day, and the lingering high clouds reflected bronze and gold. But the only light at the deserted station was a single lantern casting a dingy circle on the rough boards of the platform. Beyond the circle was the faint outline of Zack's truck in the dark; past that was only the void of the open prairie.

After a while Matthew saw a yellowish beam, far in the distance. In a few minutes it seemed larger and more white, and a few minutes after that he could hear the steam locomotive chugging toward the station. Matthew leaned against the station wall, waiting.

The train pulled in, the engine passing the platform as it slowed with squealing brakes. The lights from the train car cast flickering shadows across Matthew's haunted face. A cloud of steam enveloped his feet, mingling with the evening mists as the train came to a stop. The hiss of the air brakes and rumble of the engine were very loud.

Matthew scanned the windows of the train, but there was no sign of Zack. He walked the length of the train, but still nothing. Maybe Zack had taken a later train, he thought.

But then the door of the rear car swung open. For a moment no one emerged; then Zack appeared on the platform, carrying his carpetbag.

Matthew stood more erect but made no move toward Zack. His face was calm, but his hand opened and closed with tension.

Zack spotted Matthew standing at the edge of the pool of light. He hesitated for only a moment before he put his carpetbag down and walked over.

The set of the boy's shoulders is different, Zack thought—and was startled when Matthew looked him straight in the eye. Something had been settled, Zack knew, but he couldn't put words to it.

The two brothers stood face-to-face, each waiting for the other to speak. The silence between them grew.

Matthew squared his feet, bracing himself.

"He's dead," Matthew said. It wasn't a question.

Zack nodded affirmation.

Matthew let out a deep breath and leaned back against the station wall. Zack realized he'd been holding his own breath, as well.

"Mother said he didn't suffer at the last, except maybe in his mind," Zack said quickly. "Must have been five hundred people through that house after the funeral."

"Is Mother all right?" Matthew asked, his voice controlled.

"She's all right," Zack answered. "She sends her love."

Matthew said nothing. He picked up Zack's carpetbag, and together they walked silently to the truck as the train pulled away into the darkness.

"And him?" Matthew asked. "Did he send his love?"

Zack shrugged his shoulders. "I got there too late. He'd already left us."

Matthew looked up at his brother. "I expect that's true," he said.

Matthew tossed the carpetbag into the back of the truck. Zack got behind the wheel.

Zack studied his hands quietly; Matthew stared up

at the empty platform. In the still places of his mind, a fiddle played.

"What did you want, Matthew?" Zack asked angrily. He looked away. Beyond the bright circle of light from the platform, the prairie was dark and quiet.

Matthew stared off into the darkness for a long moment before he answered. "It's all right," he said, not looking at Zack. "*I* forgave *him*."

Matthew pulled out the crank as Zack sat behind the wheel and set the knobs and levers. On the first try, the engine caught, and Matthew got in the passenger side.

The hint of a smile touched Zack's face as he put the truck in gear and pulled away toward the ranch.

Toward home.

About the Author

Kate Seago based the story of *Matthew Unstrung* on the life of her own grandfather, who, like Matthew Hobson, suffered the horrors of the early twentieth-century mental institutions, and was lucky enough to escape to a new life out West. A newspaper editor and writer in Arizona, California, and most recently Texas, Ms. Seago has also published several short stories, and is currently at work on two more novels. In her spare time Ms. Seago enjoys gardening and needlework. She has two grown children, and lives with her husband near Dallas, Texas.